HOW NOT TO FIND YOUR LOCAL WEED MAN

HOW NOT TO FIND YOUR LOCAL WEED MAN

J. A. Springs

Copyright © 2025 Writing for the World Press, LLC.
Lancaster, PA. 17603
All rights reserved
ISBNs 13:
978-1-966464-90-7 (eBook)
978-1-966464-11-2 (Paperback)

This is a work of fiction. Names, characters, places, and incidents are the product of the author's imagination or are used fictitiously. Any resemblance to actual persons, living or dead, or actual events is purely coincidental.

For J.D.S. Let's see if your Friday's can compare.

Preface

At the time I began working on this book, I was stuck in a creative rut. I'd lost interest in reading, which had once been my escape. Even music, my other great passion, no longer held the same allure. Writing was my true love, but at that moment, I was avoiding it altogether.

I had several unfinished projects, all in different stages of completion. There was no shortage of material to work on, but one project in particular was weighing on me. I had completed the rough draft of my latest story, but it was clear that it needed significant reworking before it was ready for my first beta reader. She's someone who reads my drafts early in the process, understanding that they're rough and unfinished. Her job is to offer feedback—suggesting areas to expand or trim down—so that by the time I pass the story to an editor, it's closer to a solid first draft.

I know some authors wouldn't consider a beta reader until at least the second or third draft, after editor input. But this is just how I write. It works for me.

At the time, I was living in a city where I didn't know anyone. My only roommate worked nights, so we barely interacted. I spent most of my days alone, pondering what to do with my time. I don't like TV. I prefer activities that are purposeful—things that expand my knowledge or skills. Mindlessly zoning out to television didn't appeal to me. So, there I was, sitting and avoiding the computer, procrastinating on the rewrite I knew I needed to do, while my subconscious worked through the details that my conscious mind couldn't quite reach.

As I sat there, my mind began to wander. Thoughts floated aimlessly until one in particular stood out: *How do you meet people when you don't hang out in bars or go to clubs?* That question led to a stranger thought: *What if you smoked pot and lived in a place where you didn't know anyone?* And just like that, the seed for this novella was planted.

Chapter 1

"This is NOT how you go about finding your local 'weed man.' Trust me—I learned that the hard way."

Standing awkwardly in the parking lot of a gas station, I silently berated myself for listening to my coworkers. My first mistake? Thinking they knew what they were talking about. My second mistake? Actually acting on it. And now, here I was, staring at Darius—a guy from my high school days—leaning on his car with that easy, lopsided grin, looking like he didn't have a care in the world.

Calling Darius "sketchy" might've been unfair, but at that moment, it felt right. He had this way about him—too relaxed, too at ease with the kind of situations that would have me breaking into a cold sweat. It wasn't like we were close or anything. We'd spoken in the halls a few times, maybe traded jokes during lunch. Not strangers, but definitely not best friends.

Still, I couldn't ignore the voice of my mom in the back of my head: "Don't hang out with that boy. He's bad news." She'd said it with such certainty when she found out I'd even been acquainted with Darius. He'd gotten kicked out of our prep school during junior year. No one ever said why, and I never asked. For all I knew, it could've been anything from skipping class to something bigger.

Was my mom right about him? I wasn't sure. She had a habit of judging people she didn't know, and honestly, I never knew Darius well enough to decide for myself. What I did know was that he didn't seem to care much about what people thought of him, and that alone was enough to set him apart in a place like our high school.

And now, years later, here he was, leaning on his car like he owned the parking lot, radiating that same effortless confidence. Meanwhile, I was standing there, stiff as a board, wondering if asking him for help was the worst idea of my life or just the second-worst.

Atlanta wasn't helping my confusion. It's a city where the lines between cultures and classes blur so much they're almost invisible. You can't always tell who's who, and sometimes that's the beauty of it. Other times, like now, it's just maddening.

When people think of Atlanta, they tend to picture extremes: the mansions and Teslas of Buckhead or the chaos of a Waffle House parking lot that goes viral on TV. But Atlanta isn't all outliers. Most of the city sits somewhere in the middle—a solid, unflashy middle—where the guy fixing your AC might make as much as your cousin who's a junior accountant.

That middle makes the city hard to pin down. Sure, there's some code-switching here and there, but for the most part, people speak in a kind of shared rhythm—a linguistic gumbo that's been stewing for generations. That exaggerated "ghetto" slang you see on TV? It exists, but it's more like the bass line in a song—always there, faint and steady, but not the whole melody.

And unlike other cities where the wealthy and struggling live worlds apart, Atlanta's disparities are harder to spot. A guy in designer sneakers might be borrowing money for rent, while someone driving a beat-up pickup could own half the block. Atlanta's like that—layers of contradictions wrapped in Southern charm and big-city hustle.

I'd grown up thinking I understood this city. But standing here now, watching Darius lean against his car like he had it all figured out, I wasn't so sure anymore.

Darius, I realized, was a lot like Atlanta itself. There was more to him than met the eye, and he didn't fit neatly into any box. But that didn't stop me from labeling him as "sketchy" in my head. It was easier that way.

I hesitated, my hand hovering over my phone like it was going to give me answers. Instead, I glanced back at Darius, who raised an eyebrow at me, still grinning.

I thought to myself that this was probably a terrible idea.

Somewhere in a fancy office building downtown, I could hear Greg and Tyler now, laughing it up at their desks while I was out here wandering around Atlanta like I was on some scavenger hunt. It all started innocently enough, with a passing comment I never should have taken seriously. My mistake wasn't just listening to them—it was believing, for even a second, that their advice might actually help.

Let's back up.

I'm Malcolm Carter, your quintessential straight-laced, young Black guy from a third-generation upper-middle-class family. I work a respectable corporate job downtown, spend my days in tailored suits and shiny shoes that hurt like hell. Life is comfortable, predictable—boring, even.

Earlier that day, the madness began. The office was quiet, the kind of quiet that came after a marathon of meetings. It was during that post-meeting lull at the office I decided to get something from the canteen. Greg and Tyler had parked themselves in the break room, talking about weekend plans. I'd mentioned my date with Tasha in passing, trying to sound nonchalant.

"She's great," I'd said. "Funny, smart. Grew up in the city."

Greg's eyebrows shot up. "Oh, like Atlanta Atlanta?"

I wasn't sure what that was supposed to mean but I shrugged. "Yeah," I said, already sensing the conversation was about to take a turn.

Tyler leaned back in his chair, smirking. "Dude, you know what would make the night even better?"

I should've known. Never trust a smirk. I should've walked away right then. But no, I stayed.

"Weed," Tyler said. "Just a little something to set the mood."

Now, I don't smoke the stuff. Never have. Don't have a problem with those that do, either. But for some reason, I remembered Tasha casually mentioning how she liked to "chill" after a long day. My brain, in all its infinite wisdom, latched onto that comment and made the leap straight to weed.

Greg nodded like this was sage wisdom. "Yeah, man. Girls love it. Instant vibes."

I stared at them. "Uh, I don't... do that."

"You don't have to," Greg said, shrugging. "Just have it on hand."

"I don't even know where to get it," I offered.

Greg looked at me as if I'd put a bag of dog poop on the table. "You're telling me you don't know anyone?"

"No," I said, irritation creeping into my voice. "Why would I?"

That's when Tyler dropped the bomb. "Come on, dude. You're black. It's, like, part of the culture."

I blinked. "That is the most ridiculous thing I've ever heard."

Greg raised his hands defensively. "I mean, we're not saying you do it. We're just saying it should be... easier. Don't you have any cousins or something?"

Cousins?

The conversation had spiraled into absurdity from there, with Greg and Tyler offering increasingly unhelpful advice. By the end of it, I'd somehow convinced myself that maybe, just maybe, I could pull this off. For Tasha.

So, like any rational adult with zero experience in such matters, I listened to my coworkers. They thought it was hilarious.

"Malcolm, it's easy," Tyler had said, waving a dismissive hand. "Just ask around. Ask one of your 'peeps'. You're in Atlanta, for God's sake. Everybody knows somebody."

That's when it hit me: my white coworkers assumed I had some innate connection to the "weed man" because I'm black. Never mind that I've never touched drugs in my life. Never mind that I grew up in a pristine suburban bubble where the wildest thing we did was sneak extra dessert after dinner.

You see, my upbringing didn't exactly prepare me for this. It didn't exactly put me in close contact with anyone who knew where to find drugs, let alone sell them. My parents, third-generation upper-middle-class, raised me in a bubble of financial stability and private schooling. I don't have that one cousin who's always asking for "a little loan to hold them over." I don't have an uncle who knows a guy who knows a guy. My world growing up was structured, predictable, and—frankly—boring.

So when my coworkers started suggesting I "just ask around" to score some weed for my date with Tasha, I was completely lost. For them, it was all frat brothers and casual connections—people who dealt weed as a side hustle while working on their MBA. For me? Nothing. Zero. No frame of reference.

But instead of explaining that no, I don't have some mystical hotline to illegal substances, I nodded like an idiot. Why? Because I wanted to impress Tasha.

I looked at Tyler cross-eyed, glad that he hadn't said, 'Your People'. Even I knew what that would have meant.

I knew for a fact that he wasn't racist, nor had any inclination of the sort, but that kind of statement, heard by the other people in their cubicles, could have caused a disaster. I wondered if he knew what he'd almost done.

Greg chimed in, nodding sagely like he was a weed sage or something. "Yeah, just find one of your peeps and make it happen."

Your peeps. That phrase had clanged around in my head like a loose bolt ever since. Because, to be clear, I didn't have any 'peeps'. Not for this, anyway. But here I was, considering standing on a street corner, pretending like I was about to casually blend into a world I had zero connection to.

That said, let's talk about Tasha.

Now, here's the thing about Tasha: she grew up in the hood—her words, not mine. She mentioned it casually during one of our early conversations, like it was no big deal. With the kind of nonchalance that made me think it was just another detail about her life, like her love of oat milk or her obsession with '90s R&B. But I'd internalized it in a way I hadn't realized until now.

I'll admit, I had some preconceived notions about what that meant. I figured she'd be into certain things—one of them being weed. Turns out, I was wrong. But by the time I realized that, I was already too deep in this ridiculous mission.

It wasn't her fault. It was mine. Somewhere along the way, I'd decided I needed to bridge some imaginary gap between our worlds. I thought, Hey, maybe Tasha would think it's cool if I had some weed for our date.

Spoiler alert: I was wrong.

Tasha never mentioned weed. She didn't ask for it, hint at it, or give any indication that she cared. The idea was entirely mine—born out of my ignorance and assumptions. I thought I could somehow bridge a cultural gap that, in reality, didn't even exist.

Which brings me back to Tasha and how we met.

Tasha wasn't just another girl. She was the first person—hell, the first anything—to ever make me question the path my mom had so carefully mapped out for my life. Growing up, there was always a plan: get good grades, go to a good college, secure a good job, and eventually marry a "nice girl" who checked all the appropriate boxes. That last part? I'd never given it much thought. Not because I wasn't interested in girls—I was—but because none of them had ever stood out enough to pull my attention away from my mom's relentless vision of my "perfect" future.

And then there was Tasha.

She didn't just catch my eye; she crashed through the blinders I didn't even realize I'd been wearing, scattering my carefully organized priorities like leaves in the wind. It wasn't her beauty, though I'd be lying if I said that wasn't part of it. She was beautiful—striking in a way that made people turn their heads. But it wasn't the kind of beauty that made her seem untouchable. There was something about the way she carried herself, like she didn't care if people looked or not. She wasn't trying to impress anyone; she was just her.

And that's what made her stand out. It was effortless.

The first time I saw her, she was in line at that coffee shop, scrolling through her phone with this relaxed, almost amused expression on her face, like she was in on some private joke the rest of us weren't cool enough to understand. She ordered a caramel macchiato with oat milk and no whip, and I remember thinking how absurdly specific that was. But then, when she turned to ask me for a napkin, it didn't feel absurd at all. It felt completely normal—like it made perfect sense for someone like her to want her coffee just the way she liked it.

I was the awkward one, fumbling through a half-joke about being a "dairy rebel" while she laughed—a rich, genuine laugh that hit me like a sucker punch. It wasn't just her looks or her laugh, though. It was the way she made me feel like me. Like I wasn't just another guy in a suit, standing in line for caffeine. For the first time in a long time, I wasn't thinking about work or my mom's expectations. I was just... there.

And what really threw me was that someone like her—a woman who could have easily walked past me without a second glance, who probably had guys vying for her attention on a daily basis—actually chose me.

That was the part I couldn't quite wrap my head around.

I wasn't the guy people noticed. I wasn't the guy who stood out in a crowd or turned heads when I walked into a room. I was the guy who followed the rules, did what he was supposed to do, and stayed comfortably in his lane. And yet, there she was—this magnetic, confident, stunning woman—choosing to spend her time with me.

It wasn't just humbling; it was almost terrifying. Because what if I wasn't enough? What if she eventually realized I was just another guy in a suit, with no clue how to navigate her world?

But those thoughts only came later. In that moment, all I knew was that Tasha had changed something in me. She made me want to be the kind of guy who deserved her attention—not because I felt like I had to impress her, but because I wanted to hold onto the way she made me feel: alive, seen, and for once, enough.

We exchanged numbers, and soon after, we went out more than a few times. Tasha was smart, funny, and ridiculously kind. But she also had this edge to her—a street-smart confidence that I'd only seen in movies. She grew up in a world completely different from mine, and I'll admit it.

I remembered one night at dinner when the waiter was rattling off a list of wine recommendations that all sounded the same to me. Tasha, without missing a beat, held up a hand and said, "We'll do the Syrah, please. Great body, smooth finish." Her tone was polite but firm, her smile warm enough to disarm any sting her interruption might've caused. The waiter didn't seem annoyed—in fact, he smiled back, nodded, and walked off like he'd just been complimented.

I'd been halfway through Googling what a Syrah was when she turned to me and said, "Don't overthink it, Malcolm. Just drink what you like." Her words weren't just advice about wine—they were a window into the way she saw the world. Confident, unbothered, and completely in control, yet somehow still approachable. She had this way of making everyone feel at ease, like they were part of her orbit without her even trying.

I should probably mention something else: I've never been in a relationship before. Not once. Never held a girl's hand, never kissed, never dated. Not in high school, not even in college. And that's where I messed up. I was too laser-focused on getting my degree, with my mom constantly pushing me from behind like I was a racehorse at the Kentucky Derby. If my name had been Sea Biscuit, she'd have slapped a saddle on me and called it a day.

Back to the present. Darius raised an eyebrow again, that lopsided grin still glued to his face. It was like he knew I was stalling, daring me to either walk over or turn around and leave. I sighed, shoving my phone back into my pocket. This was probably a terrible, terrible idea.

Chapter 2

The first rule of asking for weed—as I now understood—was to not look like you were asking for weed. Unfortunately, I hadn't quite mastered that yet. My first attempt at ever finding some had me wandering the streets of Atlanta with Bradley, who, despite his corporate stiffness, had decided to tag along for his so-called 'education'. Now, I was taking a different approach. A more strategic one.

Let me take a moment to explain how Bradley got roped into this mess. He's been my best friend since college and somehow manages to work with me, Greg, and Tyler—the two geniuses responsible for the terrible advice that got me here in the first place. When Bradley overheard our break room discussion (because, of course, nothing stays private in an office), he decided to tag along. Apparently, the art of office gossip is some mystical force that defies all understanding. One minute you're venting over coffee; the next, half the floor knows about it. How it spreads so fast is beyond me.

Figuring out the secret of life—or a way to make billions by napping—would probably be easier than uncovering how gossip spreads in an office. If anyone ever managed to crack that code, they'd probably also discover the secret to harnessing perpetual motion or something.

Anyway, I decided to start at the coffee shop where I'd met Tasha. Not because it was a logical choice, but because it felt familiar. Safe, even. Plus, I figured the barista might know someone. Baristas know everything, right?

Bradley insisted on coming along, of course. Looking pale as hell, his tousled blond hair falling into his face over his glasses, he'd shown up with an espresso in one hand and what looked suspiciously like a guidebook to Atlanta in the other. "Just in case we need some direction," he'd said. I hadn't even bothered asking why he thought a guidebook would help us locate a weed man.

"You'd be surprised how often these things come in handy," Bradley had said, flipping through the pages like he was reviewing a battle plan. "I mean, it's Atlanta. You never know."

Why Bradley thought we'd need a guidebook for this kind of 'errand' was beyond me. Then again, this was the same guy who packed one for our beach trip to Savannah, just in case we needed to learn about 'local attractions'. Hell, we worked part of the year in Savannah, switching between the cities for our job.

The coffee shop was buzzing when we arrived. The usual mix of freelancers, students, and over-caffeinated moms filled the air with a hum of chatter and the hiss of the espresso machine. Bradley surveyed the scene like he was walking onto the trading floor of Wall Street.

"So, who do we ask?" he said, nudging me toward the counter.

"Let me handle this," I muttered. Bradley's version of 'subtle' was about as effective as a neon sign. Maybe even going so far as describing it as something like cheerleaders at a wake.

The barista, a guy with a man bun and tattoos of what looked like abstract coffee cups, greeted me with a smile. "What can I get you today?"

I hesitated, suddenly hyper-aware of how ridiculous this was. "Uh, actually, I was wondering if you could help me with something else."

His eyebrows lifted slightly. "Sure. What's up?"

I leaned in, trying to keep my voice low. "I... need to find someone. Someone who might be able to... provide... recreational supplies."

The barista tilted his head. "Recreational supplies? Like... a yoga mat?"

Bradley snorted behind me, and I shot him a glare. "No," I said quickly. "More like... something more like organic supplies."

The barista's face lit up with understanding, or so I thought. "Oh, gotcha. Hold on." He ducked behind the counter and came back with a business card. "These guys are great. Best landscaping service in the area. They'll handle any kind of weed situation you've got."

I stared at the card in my hand. "Landscaping?"

"Yeah, man. They're top-notch. Super professional."

"Right," I said slowly, stuffing the card in my pocket. "Thanks."

Bradley was grinning like a kid on Christmas as we stepped outside. "Well, that went well," he said, clearly enjoying my discomfort.

"Don't," I warned, but he was already laughing.

"Landscaping! You can't make this stuff up."

"I'm glad you're entertained," I muttered. "This is your fault, you know. If you hadn't insisted on tagging along—"

"Tagging along?" he interrupted. "I'm contributing! You're the one who can't ask a simple question."

We were on Peachtree Street, near the intersection with 10th. It was one of those pockets of Atlanta where upscale met laid-back, the kind of place that could only exist in this city. The coffee shop we'd just left—industrial-chic with its exposed brick walls and Edison bulbs—sat snugly between a high-end boutique with mannequins dressed in minimalist cashmere and a yoga studio advertising "detoxifying sound baths."

Across the parking lot, at the corner, sat a gas station that looked like it had been forgotten by time. Its faded sign buzzed faintly, fighting to stay lit, while the cracked pavement was littered with stray receipts, gum wrappers, and a crushed soda can or two. A single flickering bulb hung precariously over the rusted pumps, swaying gently in the afternoon breeze. Believe it or not, the place was still busy with gas buying customers.

The juxtaposition was striking. On one side of the parking lot: polished, fast-talking professionals and trendy freelancers sipping overpriced matcha lattes. On the other: a scene that could have been plucked straight from a rap video. A black Mercedes, its hood gleaming under the Atlanta sun, served as a makeshift lounge for a group of young men. Designer sneakers, flashy chains, and jeans that were either impossibly skinny or slung so low they seemed to defy gravity completed the picture. They weren't doing anything in particular—just scrolling on their phones, laughing occasionally, and soaking up the lazy vibe of a slow afternoon.

This was Atlanta for you. Only here could you find a strip mall with designer shops and artisanal coffee just a stone's throw from a gas station that looked like it belonged in an indie film about urban decay. The whole scene felt almost comical, like someone had dropped a relic of the past into a glossy, modern postcard.

I stopped mid-step as Bradley's gaze landed on them. I already knew what was coming.

"You think you can do better?" I asked, folding my arms.

Bradley's grin turned thoughtful, his confidence annoyingly intact. "You know," he said, "I probably can."

"Oh, really?"

"Yeah. You've been tiptoeing around the whole thing. If you just came out and said what you wanted, we'd be done by now."

I sighed, crossing my arms tighter. "Fine. Be my guest."

He glanced back at the group and nodded toward them like he'd found the solution to a puzzle. "Them," he said decisively.

"Nope," I said, immediately taking a step back. "Absolutely not."

But Bradley was already on the move, guidebook still tucked under his arm like he was on a walking tour. I trailed behind, partly out of curiosity and partly because I couldn't let him get himself killed—or worse, make a complete fool of both of us.

The guys noticed him approaching. One of them, dressed in a Gucci jacket and gold-rimmed sunglasses, leaned back on the hood of the car, his expression unreadable. Another adjusted his fitted cap, looking more amused than anything. They didn't seem threatened or bothered, just curious about why this clean-cut, business-casual guy was walking up to them like he was selling life insurance.

"Excuse me, gentlemen," Bradley said, his tone polite and confident, like he was asking for the nearest Whole Foods.

The group paused, their attention shifting to him. No smirks, no side-eyes. Just a casual, "What's up?"

"I was wondering," Bradley continued, completely unfazed, "if you might know where someone could, uh... procure a little greenery?" He even threw in air quotes, and I nearly buried my face in my hands. Greenery? Really?

The guy in the Gucci jacket raised an eyebrow, his lips twitching as if suppressing a laugh. "Greenery?"

"You know," Bradley said, maintaining his composure. "Weed."

One of the others shook his head with a shrug. "Nah, man. I knew someone, but he stopped selling a while back. Don't know anyone else, especially not last minute."

The others nodded in agreement, their interest in the conversation already waning.

"What's that?" Gucci Jacket asked, nodding toward Bradley's hand. His tone was casual, like he was asking about the weather.

"Oh, just a guidebook," Bradley replied, holding it up. Bradley said matter-of-factly. He offered it up like it was a business card. "Want it?"

Gucci Jacket grinned and took the guidebook, flipping through the pages with one hand while balancing his phone in the other. "Yo," he said, his grin widening as he held up the book for the others to see. "This thing's got good coupons in the back. Like, real good ones. Check this out—20% off that BBQ joint over on Peachtree. That spot is fire."

Bradley watched the men flipping the pages of the book. From where I stood, I could only gape at the absurdity of the situation. Coupons? Bradley had just handed over a guidebook to a group of guys he'd randomly approached for weed, and now they were excited about restaurant discounts.

"Unreal," I muttered under my breath.

"Appreciate it," Bradley said with a nod, like he'd just wrapped up a business deal.

I was surprised by what happened next. One of the guys reached out his hand and he and Bradley exchanged some jaw dropping, hand-slapping gestures that left me dizzy. "Thanks for your time," Bradley finished.

"No prob, bro. Keep it easy, and thanks for the book," replied the guy with the Gucci jacket.

The group shrugged again and went back to their phones as if nothing had happened. Bradley strolled back toward me, completely unbothered.

"That's it?" I asked, trying to keep my voice steady.

"That's it," he said, as calm as ever. "They don't know anyone. Why?"

I hesitated, searching for the right words. "Because... they didn't look at you funny or anything."

Bradley raised an eyebrow. "Why would they?"

I opened my mouth, then closed it again. What had I expected? For them to assume he was a cop? To laugh him off the block? Instead, they'd treated him like anyone else who might wander up and ask a random question.

Plain. Simple. Uncomplicated.

"Never mind," I muttered, shaking my head as we walked back toward the coffee shop. Meanwhile, Bradley sipped his coffee, looking as smug as ever.

"Never mind," I muttered, shaking my head.

My phone buzzed in my pocket. It was my mother, Yvonne, calling for the third time that day. I sighed and answered.

"Hi, Mom."

"Malcolm, sweetheart! Just checking in about brunch on Sunday. You haven't forgotten, have you?"

"No, Mom. I'll be there."

"Good. And don't forget to bring your new girlfriend. What's her name again? Tasha?"

"Yes, Tasha," I said, glancing around nervously. "I'll ask her."

"Wonderful. Your father and I can't wait to meet her. Oh, and Malcolm?"

"Yes?"

"Make sure you bring flowers. First impressions matter."

I groaned inwardly. "Got it, Mom."

As I hung up, the thought of Tasha meeting my parents hit me like a lead weight. My mother would have questions—lots of them—and the idea alone made my stomach churn. I hadn't even talked to Tasha about it yet. And then there was the glaring truth: she wasn't actually my girlfriend. Not officially, anyway. I'd never asked her, too scared it might be too soon, too much, or that I might come across as inadequate.

I kicked myself for casually mentioning to my mother that I was going on a date with Tasha when she'd asked me to stop by one evening. Damn, I'm such an idiot. Mom, bless her heart, latched onto the fact that her precious baby boy had found a girl and wouldn't let go. It was like watching a bulldog sink its teeth into a Tomahawk ribeye.

This fiasco was grating my nerves. It didn't help that man-bun came out of the store at that exact moment.

Man-bun—yeah, I know, not his name, but in my defense, I wasn't in the best mood. My frustration needed a target, and he just happened to step into the line of fire.

Man-bun came outside probably for a break, while I was still mentally kicking myself for how badly I'd handled this whole thing. I couldn't even be mad at him for misunderstanding me earlier—it was my fault for being vague. Still, seeing him made my irritation flare up again, even if it wasn't entirely fair.

"You guys still hanging around?" he asked, his tone light. "Need more advice?"

I froze. Bradley, of course, didn't miss a beat.

"Actually," he said, shooting me a sly glance, "we might."

I glared at him, but the barista didn't seem to notice. Bradley took a sip of his coffee, leaning casually against the wall. He looked upwards seeming to have found something interesting to look at up in the sky. I could see the smile on his face. The smug bastard. I looked back at man-bun.

"What's up?" he asked.

Bradley waited. I got the hint.

I cleared my throat, deciding to take a page out of Bradley's playbook. "So, uh... about the organic supplies."

"I hope those guys help you out," the barista smiled.

"Umm... honestly, I'm looking for something like... herbal remedies," I said. I hoped he'd get the hint. Somehow, I was still too nervous to just out and out say it like Bradley had done.

The barista's eyebrows lifted. "Oh, you're serious? It's always good to go organic."

Bradley stifled a laugh, and I pressed on, ignoring him. "Yeah. Just trying to... explore my options."

The barista nodded slowly, as if considering something. "Okay, okay. You want to check out this spot I know. Real low-key, all about natural organics."

My ears perked up. "Natural organics?"

"Yeah," he said, warming to the subject. "They've got everything—all kinds of herbal stuff. Totally organic."

I nodded, trying to play it cool. "Right. Herbal stuff. That's... exactly what I'm looking for."

He rattled off directions to a place a few blocks away. "You can't miss it," he said. "It's got a big green sign. Real earthy vibe."

"Perfect," I said, already picturing some sketchy place.

Bradley, on the other hand, looked skeptical. "You sure about this?"

"Trust me," the barista said, grinning. "It'll be worth it."

Bradley shrugged. I looked between him and the barista, thinking I'd missed some crucial bit of information.

It didn't take long to get there. It was within walking distance.

The place was not what I had imagined. For starters, it smelled like lavender and disappointment. The shelves were packed with jars of dried herbs, mysterious powders, and teas with names I couldn't pronounce.

The big sign out front should have told me something. Health Food.

"This," Bradley said, taking it all in, "is not what I expected."

"Can I help you find something?" chirped a woman in a tie-dye apron who appeared out of nowhere. She had the kind of cheerful energy that made me immediately uncomfortable.

"Uh, yeah," I said, trying to sound casual. "I'm looking for... something relaxing. Herbal."

Her face lit up. "Oh, you'll love our mugwort tea! It's great for unwinding and enhancing dreams."

"Mugwort?" I asked, suspicious. Was that code for something?

Bradley coughed. I glanced at him to find out if he was okay but he'd already walked off and the woman had started speaking again.

"And if you're looking for something a little stronger," she continued, "we have valerian root. Perfect for calming the nervous system."

"Right," I said, nodding like I understood. "Valerian root."

"And our ashwagandha powder is fantastic for stress relief," she added.

"Totally," I said. "Stress relief is... exactly what I need."

By the time I escaped with a bag of loose-leaf tea, Bradley was waiting by the door, shaking his head.

"Explain," he said, barely containing his laughter.

"What?"

"You thought this was a dispensary?" Bradley asked me.

I frowned. "What's a dispensary?"

"What's a dispensary?" Bradley smirked. "Of course you don't know. I keep forgetting you've lived your entire life in an after-school special."

The blank look was obviously still stuck on my face because Bradley stared at me like I'd just asked what water was.

"A dispensary. You know, where people buy weed legally. With labels. And receipts," he continued.

"Receipts?"

"Yes, Malcolm. Receipts. It's not like some shady back alley deal. It's a business."

I gripped the bag of tea tighter, trying to salvage what little dignity I had left. "Well, excuse me for not knowing the finer details of weed commerce."

Bradley burst out laughing, nearly doubling over as we started walking again, and my mind spun. How had Bradley's approach worked so smoothly? Sure, it didn't lead anywhere, but the way they'd responded to him was so... normal. Like he wasn't the awkward corporate guy I knew him to be. Meanwhile, I couldn't even manage to get through a basic conversation without looking like I'd wandered into the wrong movie set.

I ended up getting a damn tea I didn't even need. Nor want.

Bradley sarcastically muttered, "This is why you're better at spreadsheets than scavenger hunts,"

I guessed that he was right. I had no business out here looking for a weed man.

He then followed it up with, "Alright, let's think. Who do you know that's a little less... wholesome? Someone who knows the scene better than you, obviously."

I looked over at him blankly. Didn't expect the question.

And then it hit me.

Darius.

"Someone who knows the scene," Bradley had said. The words stuck with me. It wasn't like I didn't know someone who used to fit that description. Darius came to mind, uninvited, his easy grin flashing like a warning sign from the past. I brushed the thought aside. That guy was supposedly trouble, and I didn't need more of it right now. Right?"

The memory came out of nowhere, like flipping a switch.

Back in high school, Darius was always the person who had a solution for everything, even when you didn't need one. Darius had been the guy who always knew a guy. Tickets to a sold-out concert? Darius knew someone. Trouble with a teacher? Darius could talk his way out of anything. If anyone could point me in the right direction, it was him.

We'd drifted apart over the years, but if anyone could point me in the right direction, it was him. Still, calling him felt like digging up a part of my past I'd buried along with my childhood sneakers.

I pulled out my phone and scrolled through my contacts, the name jumping out at me like it'd been waiting for this moment. Darius. My thumb hovered over his number, the hesitation thick in my chest. Was this even still a good number to reach him? I'd gotten the number a few months ago after running into someone while pumping gas. He told me Darius asked about me and gave me his number.

I hovered my thumb over the number, then slid the phone back into my pocket.

"Got an idea," I said, mostly to myself.

Bradley gave me a side-eye. "You gonna share with the class?"

"Not yet," I said. "But I might know someone who can help."

We'd barely made it back to the car before doubt started creeping in.

"You sure this is a good idea?" I asked, leaning against the passenger door.

Bradley gave me one of his patented seriously? looks as he unlocked the car. "Malcolm, what you're trying to do is not rocket science. You just have to find the right person to ask."

I snorted. "Yeah, because that's been working out so well."

He shrugged as he climbed in. "The problem isn't the asking, it's who you're asking. You just have to find someone who knows the scene. That's it."

Someone who knows the scene. The words stuck with me as I got into the car. It wasn't like I didn't know someone, or at least, used to know someone. Darius.

The name popped into my head again, along with a flood of memories. Darius with his crooked grin, always a little too smooth for his own good. The guy who could sweet-talk his way out of detention, but who also got suspended junior year for reasons no one ever really nailed down.

I could practically hear my parents' voices from back then.

"You need to stop hanging around boys like that, Malcolm. People judge you by the company you keep."

"He's not your friend; he's trouble, and you know it."

Trouble. That was always their word for him. But trouble or not, Darius always had my back. And if anyone could help me figure this out, it was him.

Still, I hesitated, my thumb hovering over his number in my contacts. It'd been years since we talked. For all I knew, he'd laugh in my face—or worse, he wouldn't even remember me.

"What's the hold-up?" Bradley asked, glancing at me as he started the car.

I shoved my phone into my pocket. "Nothing," I muttered.

But it wasn't nothing. I was standing on the edge of something, and the only way to move forward was to jump.

I took a deep breath. You're an adult now. Your parents don't get to decide who you talk to.

Pulling out my phone again, I pressed the call button before I could change my mind.

The line rang twice before a voice answered.

"Yo, this is D."

"Uh, hey, Darius. It's Malcolm."

There was a pause, long enough for me to wonder if he'd hung up.

"Malcolm?" His voice lit up with recognition. "Man, it's been a minute! What's good?"

I laughed nervously, the sound hollow even to me. "Yeah, it's been a while. I was just thinking, you know, about old times. Thought I'd give you a call, see how you're doing."

"You serious?" he asked, and I could hear the smile in his voice. "Outta nowhere, huh?"

"Yeah," I said, the lie slipping out too easily. "Been meaning to reach out. Just, uh... you know how it is. Life."

"Sure, sure," he said. "What's up, though? Something on your mind?"

"No, no," I stammered. "Nothing like that. Just... wanted to catch up."

The silence on the line stretched for a moment, but Darius didn't press me. I exhaled slowly and felt it as my shoulders sagged.

"Well, I'm on my way to work right now, but I've got a little time. You in the area? We could link up for a minute."

"Yeah, yeah, that'd be great," I said, relief flooding my voice.

He gave me quick directions to a gas station not far from his job.

"See you there," he said, and the call ended.

I let out a breath I hadn't realized I was holding.

"What'd he say?" Bradley asked, glancing over as he drove.

"He said he's got a minute," I replied.

Bradley nodded like it was the most obvious thing in the world. "See? Easy, peasy."

Easy for him to say. My stomach was already tying itself in knots.

Chapter 3

The gas station where Darius told me to meet him was one of those spots where the fluorescent lights buzzed just a little too loudly, and the windows were plastered with ads for discount cigarettes and lottery tickets. The canceled tickets of big winners were pasted on display, the sunlight having already faded the ink to near illegibility.

The faint smell of motor oil hung in the air, barely masking the overwhelming stench of gasoline. As I pulled in, I spotted Darius leaning casually against his car, scrolling through his phone like he didn't have a care in the world.

"Malcolm," he called out when he saw me, his grin widening. "Man, it's been forever! You clean up nice." He gestured at my button-up shirt and slacks.

"Hey, Darius," I said, trying to sound more relaxed than I felt.

"What brings you out here?" he asked, his eyes narrowing slightly, like he already knew there was more to this than I was letting on.

I hesitated just a beat too long. "Just... thought we could catch up. You know, like old times."

"Uh-huh." He tilted his head, not buying it for a second. "Well, I've got a few minutes before I gotta head in. What's really going on?"

Before I could scramble for an excuse, Bradley stepped out of the car, looking Darius up and down like he was appraising him for a job interview. "So this is Darius?" he said. "Nice to meet you."

Darius raised an eyebrow, his grin shifting to something a little more amused. "And you are?"

"Bradley," I said quickly. "Coworker. He, uh... wanted to come along."

To my surprise, Darius laughed. "Alright, Bradley. You a friend of Malcolm's, you're cool with me."

"Appreciate it," Bradley said, sticking out his hand. Darius shook it, and their handshake was this intricate mix of claps, snaps, and fist bumps that I'd never seen before. It was the kind of handshake that screamed we're on the same wavelength, and I felt like an outsider watching it. Cool.

"So, what's up?" Bradley asked Darius, leaning against the car like they'd been buddies for years.

"Not much," Darius said with a shrug. "Just working, staying out of trouble. You?"

"Same," Bradley replied. "You know how it is."

I stood there awkwardly as they bantered about random stuff—football, bad drivers, gas prices—like they'd known each other forever. Meanwhile, I couldn't help but wonder how Bradley managed to fit in so effortlessly. Wasn't I supposed to be the one who knew Darius? Yet somehow, he was the one who looked like he belonged.

Darius and I went way back—high school, to be exact. It wasn't like we were best friends or anything, but we had a history. I still remembered the day he walked up to me out of nowhere, introducing himself like we were already friends. I'd been hesitant. Everyone had said vague things about him—not bad, exactly, but not good, either. But Darius? He moved through life so easily, like he belonged everywhere. I'd always admired that about him.

Finally, I blurted out, "So, Darius, what are you up to these days?"

He gave me a look that said Finally, a real question. Crossing his arms, he leaned back against his car and said, "I'm a GS-11."

I blinked. "A GS-11?"

Bradley's eyebrows shot up. "That's a solid spot. Mixed telework?"

"Yeah," Darius said with a nod. "Couple days in the office, couple at home. Army reserves opened the door, you know? After that, I landed some good GS work."

I stared at him, my brain scrambling to catch up. "Wait, you're a government employee? Like... official?"

Darius smirked. "What did you think I was doing? Still hustling in the streets?"

"I... I don't know," I stammered. "I just didn't expect... this."

"People grow, man," he said, pointing at me with a grin.

I glanced down at his worn jeans and plain T-shirt. "So... you dress like that for work?"

"Depends on the day," he said, shrugging. "Telework's a blessing. When I'm in the office, it's business casual. Ties choke me out."

I looked down at my own shiny shoes, the gas station's fluorescent lights reflecting off the leather. My toes ached in the tight confines, and suddenly, I felt ridiculous. My parents' voices echoed in my head, from all those years ago: "Darius isn't your kind of friend, Malcolm. You need to focus on people who'll help you get ahead." I'd let them shape how I saw him, how I saw myself. And here he was, doing better than I ever gave him credit for.

"Anyway," Darius said, snapping me out of my thoughts, "it pays the bills, and it's steady. I've got my benefits, my time off, and my weekends. You can't beat that."

"No, you really can't," Bradley said, nodding like he'd just found his new role model. "Props, man."

"Appreciate it," Darius replied, his grin widening. "So, Malcolm, what about you? Still chasing spreadsheets?"

"Uh, yeah," I said, feeling suddenly self-conscious. "Corporate work. You know how it is."

Darius chuckled. "Yeah, I've heard. Seems like you're doing alright for yourself."

Their conversation paused when a girl walked past us, heading into the gas station. She was stunning, her long legs emphasized by a fitted dress, and she moved with the kind of confidence that turned heads. Darius whistled low, and Bradley let out a soft, "Damn."

"You see that?" Darius asked, nudging Bradley with his elbow.

"I saw that," Bradley said, grinning. "How the hell could I miss it? She definitely wasn't here for the gas."

They both laughed, clapping each other on the shoulder like old friends. I stood there awkwardly, unsure whether to join in or wait it out.

As the girl disappeared into the store, Darius turned back to me, still smiling. "Alright, Malcolm. Let's put the bullshit aside. What's really going on?"

I sighed, realizing I wasn't going to get out of this without some honesty. "Look, I need to find... something. And I thought maybe you could help."

"Something?" Darius said, his grin widening. "What kind of something?"

"You know," I muttered, lowering my voice. "Weed."

Darius threw his head back and laughed so loudly that a guy filling up his truck turned to stare. "You? Trying to buy weed? Man, I did not see that coming."

"Keep it down," I hissed.

Darius cut me off. "Why? Don't nobody care."

I looked around cautiously, not really believing what he'd just said. "Can you help or not?" I asked, my face burning.

"Relax," Darius said, still chuckling. "Yeah, I know someone. Come on."

The neighborhood Darius drove us to wasn't exactly what I'd call welcoming. The buildings were old and a little run-down, and the streets were littered with potholes and faded graffiti. Bradley, to his credit, didn't say a word, but I could see his eyes darting around, taking in every detail like he was on a field trip.

"Here we are," Darius said, pulling up in front of a bodega with bars on the windows. The sign above the door flickered weakly, and the paint was peeling off the walls.

"This is it?" I asked, already regretting every decision that had led me to this moment.

"Trust me," Darius said with a wink. "Uncle Leroy's got what you need."

Inside the bodega, the smell of stale chips and overripe bananas hit me like a wall. Behind the counter was an older man in a stained T-shirt, his sharp eyes narrowing as he took us in. Uncle Leroy stood up from the stool he'd been sitting on.

"What you want?" he asked, his tone making it clear he wasn't here for small talk.

Darius stepped up confidently. "Uncle Leroy, this is my boy Malcolm. He's looking for something."

I swallowed hard, questioning every life choice that had led me to this exact moment. What was I even doing here? All this just to impress Tasha? I didn't even know if she smoked weed, and here I was, sweating under the fluorescent lights, feeling like a suspect in a bad cop show.

Leroy's gaze locked on me, zeroing in on my pressed clothes and nervous expression. "You a cop?" he asked bluntly.

"What? No!" I said, my voice cracking slightly. "I'm not a cop."

Leroy leaned forward, his eyes narrowing even further. "You sure? 'Cause you look like a cop. All nervous and dressed up like that."

"I'm not a cop," I repeated, trying to sound more convincing. "I'm just here to..."

"Hey, now," Bradley interjected, stepping forward. "Let's not jump to conclusions. My friend is just—"

"Who's this?" Leroy cut him off, pointing a finger at Bradley.

"Coworker," Darius said quickly, clearly trying to defuse the situation.

Leroy didn't look convinced. His eyes narrowed further, and I felt the room shrink around me. Oh great, now I'm about to get kicked out of a bodega—or worse. All this for something I wasn't even sure I'd use. He reached under the counter, and I heard the unmistakable sound of a button being pressed.

My stomach dropped.

"I don't like liars," he said.

Within seconds, a large man who could've doubled as a bouncer appeared from the back room.

"What's the problem, Leroy?" the man rumbled.

"This one looks like an undercover. Says he's not a cop, but I don't buy it," Leroy said, pointing at me. "And this one..." He pointed at Bradley. "This one's just asking too many questions. Being too damn nosey."

"Whoa, whoa, whoa," Bradley said, holding up his hands. "I'm not asking questions. I'm just here to experience... uh, local culture."

"Local culture?" the bouncer repeated, his eyebrows lifting in disbelief. The bouncer turned his gaze on me, and I felt the room shrink around me. "You don't look local," he said, his deep voice making my knees weak.

Darius stepped in, his tone easy and relaxed. "Derrick, chill. He's good. He's just... new to all this."

Derrick didn't look convinced. "You vouching for him?"

"Yeah," Darius said without hesitation. "He's my guy."

There was a long pause before Derrick finally nodded, his eyes still locked on me. "Alright, but if you're lying..."

"I'm not," Darius said quickly, his voice steady. "We're cool."

Derrick's gaze lingered on me for an agonizing moment before he finally stepped back, his broad shoulders still blocking half the room. "Just don't waste Leroy's time," he said, his tone leaving no room for argument.

I exhaled slowly, the knot in my chest loosening—until Bradley, in his infinite wisdom, decided that things were going absolutely splendid and thought, Why not toss a brick into the mix to make this just... perfect?

"How can you say I'm asking too many questions? I'm just here to see more of the city. That's what this is about, right? Experiencing the local culture," he stated.

Damn it, Bradley, I thought, the blood draining from my face. This isn't a field trip.

Derrick's expression hardened, his eyes narrowing as he turned his full attention to Bradley. "Local culture?" he repeated, his voice low and dangerous.

"Yeah," Bradley said, oblivious to the warning signs. "You know, just getting a feel for the real Atlanta."

I clenched my fists, resisting the urge to physically drag him out of there. "Darius," I hissed under my breath, my voice barely audible, "can we go? Now."

But before Darius could respond, Derrick took a deliberate step forward, grabbing Bradley by the arm with a grip that made my stomach drop. "You need to leave," Derrick said firmly, his tone making it clear this wasn't a suggestion.

Bradley froze, his bravado faltering as he finally seemed to realize he'd pushed too far. "Unhand me," he stammered, attempting to yank his arm back. "I didn't mean—"

"We're leaving!" Darius cut in, his voice sharp as he stepped between Derrick and Bradley. "Thanks for your time, Derrick. Appreciate you, Uncle Leroy." Without waiting for a response, he grabbed Bradley's other arm and gave me a pointed look. "Let's go, Malcolm. Now."

Outside, Darius burst out laughing. "Man, y'all are something else."

"This isn't funny!" I snapped, my heart still racing. "He thought I was a cop!"

"Well, you do look like one," Darius said, smirking. "All clean-cut and jumpy."

"And what about me?" Bradley demanded. "I was just trying to engage in meaningful dialogue."

"Dialogue?" A deep voice interrupted. We turned to see the bouncer—Derrick, apparently—standing in the doorway, his expression softer now but still wary. "Man, you're lucky Leroy didn't call the cops for real."

Derrick followed us out, shaking his head as he looked me over, his expression somewhere between pity and disbelief.

"He didn't need to," I said, bristling. "I'm not undercover." I could practically hear him thinking, 'This guy can't be serious.' Honestly, I couldn't blame him. I didn't belong here, and it showed.

Derrick looked me over, his eyes narrowing slightly before flicking back to Bradley. "You, though," he said to Bradley. "You're alright. You know how to talk to people."

I blinked, incredulous. How did we go from nearly being tossed out by a guy who looked like he wrestled bears in his spare time to Bradley getting a gold star for his people skills?

Inside the bodega, I'd been one misplaced word away from getting us thrown into the back alley—or worse—and yet somehow, out here, the vibe had completely shifted. Derrick, who had glared at me like I'd shown up to the wrong class, was now practically patting Bradley on the back.

What alternate universe did I just step into? I thought, glancing at Bradley, who, of course, wore that smug, satisfied grin like he'd solved world peace. The contrast was almost comical: inside, I was the nervous outsider, while Bradley was the clueless sidekick; out here, Bradley was the smooth diplomat, and I was... well, still the nervous outsider.

It didn't make sense. But then again, nothing about this day really did.

Derrick turned to me. "Man, you've got to loosen up," Derrick said, almost sadly, before turning his attention to Darius.

I felt my stomach sink at the casual dismissal, and my grip tightened on my phone. Bradley, of course, just nodded like he'd been given a medal.

"What were y'all even here for?" Derrick asked, turning to Darius.

Darius shrugged. "Weed. Malcolm's looking."

Derrick let out a low chuckle. "Man, y'all got the wrong spot. We don't do that here no more. Cops been breathing down our necks, so Leroy shut it down. Can't help ya."

"Fair," Darius said, clapping Derrick on the shoulder. "Appreciate you, though."

My phone buzzed in my pocket. Without thinking, I answered on speaker phone. "Hello?"

"Malcolm," my mom's voice snapped. "Where are you?"

I froze. "Uh... just catching up with Darius."

"Darius?" she said sharply. "I thought we agreed he wasn't a good influence on you. Are you seriously with him right now?"

I winced. "Mom, it's fine. I'm an adult—"

"Adult or not, you should know better! He got suspended for a reason, Malcolm!"

"I really have to go," I said quickly, cutting her off. "I'll call you later."

I hung up, my face burning as I looked up to see all three of them staring at me. Bradley's shit-eating grin was back in full force, and I suddenly wished the ground would swallow me whole.

"Y'all looking for weed, huh?" Derrick spoke up. "You should've just hit up Big Tony. You know he's always got connections."

Darius snapped his fingers. "Big Tony! That's right. Damn, I didn't even think of him."

"Who's Big Tony?" I asked, trying to sound casual, though my unease was probably obvious.

Derrick smirked but didn't bother answering me. He focused on Darius instead. "Look, Tony's your best bet, but you didn't hear that from me. And Leroy's right—we had to stop keeping anything here. Cops been breathing down our necks too much."

Darius nodded. "Appreciate you, Derrick. You've always been solid."

"You got it," Derrick said, giving Darius a firm handshake.

While Darius and Derrick were still chatting and Bradley was busy basking in his newfound street cred, my phone buzzed again. For a second, I thought it was my mom calling back to yell at me some more, but when I glanced at the screen, it was Tasha.

I hesitated before picking up. Out of habit, I answered on speaker phone—again.

"Hey, Tasha," I said, trying to sound casual.

"Hey, Malcolm," she said, her voice warm and light. "Just checking—we're still on for tonight, right?"

"Oh, absolutely. I'm stoked to have dinner with you," I said, maybe too quickly.

"Cool," she said. There was a pause, then, "What are we having?"

I froze. I hadn't figured that part out yet. "Uh... I was thinking something simple. Maybe pasta?"

In the background, Darius, who'd been half-listening to my side of the conversation, suddenly said, "Man, oxtails are where it's at. I can't wait for dinner tonight. That's what I'm having."

I shot him a look that could have melted steel, but it was too late.

"Oxtails?" Tasha asked, her tone shifting into something much more interested. "Wait—you're making oxtails? I love oxtails!"

"No—uh—" I stammered, but Darius grinned and gave me a thumbs up like he'd just saved my life.

'You asshole,' I mouthed towards him.

"I didn't know you could cook oxtails," Tasha continued, sounding genuinely impressed. "That's so sweet of you."

"Yeah," I said weakly. "Sweet."

"Well, now I'm really excited for dinner. I'll see you tonight!" she said before hanging up.

I lowered the phone and glared at Darius. "Oxtails?"

"Dude, it's a classic," he said, still grinning.

"I don't even know how to make oxtails!"

"Don't look at me," Darius said, holding up his hands. "You're the one trying to impress her."

Bradley clapped me on the shoulder, his grin widening. "You'll figure it out. Just YouTube it or something."

Darius checked his watch and winced. "Man, I'd love to help you more, but I've got to get to work. Tell you what—I'll call Big Tony and set something up for later. I'll hit you up when I'm free."

I nodded, trying to keep the relief off my face. "Thanks, Darius."

"No problem," he said with a grin. "Just try to chill out, Malcolm. You're way too uptight."

Derrick, still standing in the doorway, shook his head slowly, his expression somewhere between disappointment and amusement, as he looked me over. "Man, you're tense," he said, almost sadly. "You're gonna pop one day."

I opened my mouth to respond, but Derrick waved me off and turned back to Darius. "Should've just gone to Big Tony. You know he always knows a few people who can hook you up."

Darius smacked his forehead. "That's the move."

Derrick smirked. "Just don't go wasting his time."

Derrick gave a small shrug. "Just don't come back here with the same nonsense." He clapped Darius on the shoulder and headed back inside the store, muttering something under his breath about how he didn't get paid enough for this.

Darius turned back to me, still grinning. "Alright, Malcolm, looks like we've got a lead."

I sighed, rubbing my temples. "We?"

"Yeah, we," Darius said, throwing an arm over my shoulder. "You're not bailing on this now. But..." He glanced at his watch and winced. "I gotta bounce. Work's calling, but don't worry—I'll hit you up later after I talk to Tony. He owes me a favor or two."

I nodded, though my stomach was still in knots. "Thanks, man."

"No problem," Darius said with a wink. "You just try not to embarrass yourself in the meantime." He hopped into his car and drove off, leaving me alone with Bradley.

"Big Tony, huh?" Bradley said, grinning. "This should be interesting."

I groaned, pulling out my phone and scrolling through my contacts, just in case Darius flaked. That's when I realized my mom had texted me three times in the last ten minutes. I was just about to respond when the phone buzzed in my hand again.

"Hello?" I said, already regretting it.

"Malcolm," my mom's voice snapped. "Are you still with that Darius boy?"

"No, Mom," I said quickly, trying to keep my tone even. "I'm not with him anymore. We... caught up for a bit, and now I'm with a coworker."

"You're sure you're not still running around with him? Because I don't want to hear about you getting into trouble," she said, her voice still sharp but a little less accusatory.

"I'm sure," I said, sighing. "Everything's fine."

"Good. Just remember, Malcolm, you've got that brunch on Sunday, and we'll be expecting to meet this new girlfriend of yours."

"Got it, Mom," I said, desperate to end the conversation. "I'll call you later."

I hung up and glanced at Bradley, who was staring at me with that same smug grin plastered across his face.

"What?" I snapped.

"Nothing," he said, barely containing his laughter. "You're just really good at making this harder than it needs to be."

Chapter 4

Bradley dropped me off at the office so I could grab my car, and by the time I was driving home, my brain was in overdrive. The words "Big Tony" and "oxtails" played on a loop in my head, weaving together in a chaotic mantra. I muttered to myself as I navigated through the early evening traffic, my hands gripping the steering wheel like it was the only thing keeping me grounded.

"Oxtails," I said under my breath, my voice dripping with disbelief. "Who just casually decides to make oxtails? I've never even seen oxtails at a grocery store. Do they even sell them in normal places?"

The thought of stopping at a butcher's shop was intimidating enough, but the bigger question was why I'd even agreed to this in the first place. Tasha had sounded so excited, and Darius's smug thumbs-up replayed in my mind, further cementing my irritation. He wasn't even going to be there, so why did his opinion matter?

Then there was the other issue. The weed.

"How is this so hard?" I groaned. "Every show, every movie with even a hint of urban life has people smoking a blunt like it's nothing. But no, I'm running around Atlanta like I'm on some treasure hunt—and I don't even have a damn map!"

The absurdity of the situation hit me like a wave, and for a brief moment, I debated scrapping the entire plan. Tasha didn't need weed. She'd never even mentioned it. For all I knew, she didn't smoke at all. And yet, here I was, juggling a doomed attempt to channel Gordon Ramsay while also trying to play the cool, laid-back boyfriend who totally knew his way around the local "weed man" scene.

As I pulled into my apartment complex, my stomach churned with a mix of anxiety and hunger. I parked the car and sat for a moment, staring at the dashboard. I looked over in the passenger seat to see the bag of groceries I'd stopped to get before getting home. The evening was already spiraling, and I hadn't even started cooking yet. With a resigned sigh, I grabbed my phone and started searching for YouTube tutorials on how to make oxtails before deciding I should do that in the kitchen.

Standing in my kitchen, I stared at the package of oxtails sitting on the counter like it was a foreign artifact. I had managed to find them—thankfully—but now I was realizing just how unprepared I was for this endeavor. My laptop sat open on the kitchen island, playing a video of a cheerful woman who made it look deceptively simple.

"First, you're gonna want to season them thoroughly," the woman on the screen chirped. "Don't be shy with your spices!"

I glanced down at the array of spices I had managed to scrounge up from the back of my cabinets. Most of them were questionably old, and I wasn't entirely sure they'd do anything to enhance the flavor. Still, I followed her instructions, sprinkling salt, pepper, garlic powder, and... paprika? Sure, why not.

"Next, you're gonna brown them in a hot pan. Get a nice sear on all sides!"

I turned on the stove and waited for the pan to heat up, feeling more like a contestant on a cooking competition than someone preparing for a date. The smell of sizzling meat soon filled the kitchen, and for a moment, I felt a tiny spark of confidence. Maybe I could actually pull this off.

Then my phone buzzed.

I glanced at the screen, half expecting it to be my mom again. Instead, it was a text from Tasha.

"Can't wait to see you tonight! Hope you're not going through too much trouble :)"

Too much trouble? I stared at the text, resisting the urge to laugh hysterically. This wasn't just trouble; it was a full-blown crisis. But I couldn't tell her that. Instead, I typed back a quick response.

"Everything's great! See you soon!"

The moment I hit send, the pan started smoking. "Damn it!" I yelped, grabbing a towel to wave at the smoke detector as it began to shriek. The cheerful woman on the YouTube video kept talking as if nothing was happening, her calm demeanor only fueling my frustration.

I went to add oregano to the pot but realized, with horror, that I didn't have any. Desperate, I rummaged through my spice rack and found a jar of sage. It's green, I thought. Close enough. I dumped a healthy amount into the pot, hoping it wouldn't ruin the entire dish.

An hour later, the oxtails were simmering in a pot, and my kitchen looked like a war zone. Every counter was covered with discarded utensils, spice containers, and a few unidentifiable splatters. I leaned against the sink, wiping sweat from my forehead, when my phone buzzed again.

This time, it was my mom. Again.

"Malcolm, I need to know what time brunch is on Sunday," she said the moment I answered.

"Mom, it's the same time as always," I replied, trying to keep the exasperation out of my voice.

"And you're bringing Tasha, right?"

"Yes, Mom," I said, stirring the pot distractedly.

"Good. Because I've already told everyone about her, and I don't want any surprises."

I froze. "Wait—everyone? I thought it was just going to be you and Dad."

"Oh, did I forget to mention that?" she said, her tone way too casual for what she'd just dropped. "Your cousins are coming, and Aunt Lorraine, and a few others. It's not a big deal."

"Not a big deal?" I groaned. "Mom, you could have at least warned me!"

"Don't be so dramatic, Malcolm. I wanted to show off my son's new girlfriend. You've never been in a real relationship before, and I'm proud of you."

"Awesome," I muttered. "Can't wait."

As the call ended, I stared at my phone. Why did my love life have to be everyone's business? Couldn't I date someone without feeling like I was being scrutinized under a microscope? Between brunch, the oxtails, and the weed, I was starting to feel like a contestant on a reality show where the only prize was survival.

I pushed the thought aside and went back to the stove, checking the pot. The smell wasn't terrible—promising, even. But I couldn't shake the nagging feeling that something was off. Shaking my head, I decided to focus on the next challenge: getting dressed for dinner.

As I stood in front of my closet, my phone buzzed again. This time, it was Tasha.

"Hey, Malcolm," she said when I answered. "I know I was going to wait until dinner, but... I think we need to talk now."

My heart skipped a beat. "Uh, okay. What's up?"

She paused, and I could hear her take a deep breath. "I just... I wanted to ask you something. And I didn't want to wait because, well, if this conversation doesn't go how I'm hoping, I'd rather not sit through an awkward dinner."

I sat down on the edge of the bed, my stomach knotting. "Alright," I said cautiously. "What do you want to ask?"

"Do you want to be in a serious relationship with me?" she asked, her tone direct but uncertain. "Like, an actual boyfriend-girlfriend thing?"

I blinked, caught off guard. "Wait, I thought we already were?"

She let out a small laugh, a mix of relief and amusement. "You thought we were? Malcolm, you never actually said it. I wasn't sure if you saw me that way or if we were just... hanging out."

"Of course I see you that way," I said quickly. "I mean, I just assumed... but yeah. Definitely."

"Okay," she said, and I could hear the smile in her voice. "Good. I'm glad we cleared that up."

"Me too," I said, letting out a breath I hadn't realized I was holding. "I, uh, actually wanted to tell you about something, too."

"Oh? What's that?"

I rubbed the back of my neck, suddenly feeling awkward. "Well, my mom invited you to brunch on Sunday. With my family."

There was a brief silence. "Your whole family?"

"Yeah," I admitted. "And just so you know, I'm not entirely sure how this is going to go. My family... they're a little intense."

To my surprise, she laughed. "Malcolm, it's brunch. I'm sure I can handle it."

Her confidence was reassuring, but it didn't completely ease my nerves. "I just don't want you to feel uncomfortable."

"I won't," she said firmly. "I think it's sweet that your mom wants me to come."

"You might not feel that way after you meet my Aunt Lorraine," I muttered.

"I'll take my chances," she said lightly. "Now stop worrying so much and get ready for tonight. I can't wait to see you."

"Can't wait to see you either," I said, a small smile creeping onto my face as I hung up.

The oxtails were simmering, the kitchen was mostly intact, and I'd officially been promoted to boyfriend. Now I just had to survive brunch, impress Tasha, and figure out what the hell 'local culture' even meant. Easy.

Chapter 5

Halfway through scrubbing the mountain of dishes that had accumulated in my sink, my phone buzzed on the counter. I dried my hands on a dish towel and picked it up, relieved to see an unfamiliar number rather than another call from my mom. I hesitated for a second, then answered.

"Hello?"

"Yo, this Malcolm?" a deep, smooth voice asked.

"Yeah, who's this?"

"Big Tony. Darius told me to give you a shout-out. Said you needed somethin' handled."

I blinked in surprise. "Oh, uh, yeah! Thanks for calling."

"No problem, man. Where you at? I'll swing by."

The ease in his tone threw me off for a moment, but I quickly rattled off my address.

"I'll be there in about fifteen," he replied.

"Thanks, man. I'll see you soon."

As soon as the call ended, I felt a wave of relief. Finally, things were starting to fall into place. Not wanting to waste any time, I grabbed my keys and dashed out of the apartment to hit the ATM. If movies and TV had taught me anything, it was that cash was king in these kinds of transactions. I wasn't sure how much to bring, so I withdrew $200 just to be safe.

On the way back home, I couldn't help but feel a little proud of myself. Sure, it had been a chaotic day, but I was finally getting things under control. The oxtails were simmering, the kitchen was halfway clean, and soon, I'd have the final piece of the puzzle that had started this whole mess. Things were looking up.

As I pulled into my parking spot, a sleek black SUV rolled in behind me. The driver's side door opened, and a broad-shouldered man in a crisp polo shirt stepped out, carrying a bag slung over one shoulder. Big Tony.

"You Malcolm?" he asked, flashing a friendly smile.

"Yeah, that's me," I said, holding up the cash. "Thanks for coming out."

He waved me off. "No problem, man. Let's handle this inside."

We headed up to my apartment, and I couldn't help but feel a little nervous. I'd never done this before, and I wasn't entirely sure how it was supposed to go down. Once we were inside, I turned to Big Tony and hesitated. "So, uh... how do we do this?"

He chuckled, setting his bag down on the kitchen table. "Man, it's easy. Just grab a chair and set up near some good light."

Confused, I glanced around the room. "Light?"

"Yeah, I need to see what I'm workin' with," he said, unzipping the bag.

My eyes widened as I caught a glimpse of chrome glinting in the light. My heart jumped into my throat. Oh my God, is that a gun?

I stumbled back, nearly knocking over a chair. "Whoa, whoa! What—"

Big Tony froze, then burst out laughing.

My confusion deepened as he pulled out... hair clippers.

"Man, what'd you think this was? Relax, it's just for your head!" he continued laughing.

I felt my face heat up as I realized my mistake. "Oh. Right. Clippers. Of course."

Big Tony shook his head, still chuckling. "You're wound tighter than a pocket watch, man. Sit down before you hurt yourself."

"Wait," I said slowly. "What's going on here?"

Big Tony looked up, his brow furrowing. "I'm a mobile barber, man. Darius didn't tell you?"

The realization hit me like a ton of bricks. "You're... a barber?"

"Yeah. Best in the city," he said proudly. "Darius said you needed a hookup, so I figured you were due for a fresh cut."

"Oh," I said weakly, my face heating up. "I, uh, thought... never mind."

Before I could explain the misunderstanding, the doorbell rang. I opened it to find Bradley standing there, his usual smug grin firmly in place.

"What's up, Malcolm?" he asked, stepping inside. He froze as his eyes landed on Big Tony, who was holding the clippers like a weapon. "Whoa, what's going on here?"

For a split second, I panicked. "It's... not what it looks like."

"You sure?" Bradley asked, raising an eyebrow. "Because it looks like you're about to get a haircut in your kitchen."

Embarrassed, I slumped into a chair as he plugged in the clippers. The buzz filled the room, loud and persistent, and my anxiety ratcheted up another notch. I'd never had a haircut in my kitchen before, and the whole situation felt absurd.

I couldn't figure out why getting weed would require me to get a haircut. I guessed that maybe this was some new thing I wasn't aware of. There was also now Bradley to deal with.

Big Tony laughed. "Man, your boy here didn't know what Darius meant when he said I'd hook him up. But don't worry, I'll get him lookin' right."

"A haircut?" Bradley repeated, clearly struggling to hold back laughter. "You're really going all out for this date, huh?"

I groaned, running a hand over my face. "It's not like that."

"Sure it's not," Bradley said, dropping into a chair. "I'm staying for this."

Big Tony clapped me on the shoulder. "Don't stress, man. By the time I'm done, you'll be ready for the cover of GQ. Now grab a seat and let me work my magic."

Resigned to my fate, I sat down and let Big Tony get started. As the clippers buzzed to life, I couldn't help but think about how far off-track this day had gone. All I wanted was some weed. Now, I was getting a haircut in my kitchen with Bradley providing live commentary.

Before I could think about it any further, Big Tony began asking his own quesions.

"So, how you know Darius?" Big Tony asked, his tone casual as he tilted my head to the side.

"We went to school together," I said, trying to ignore the vibrations of the clippers against my scalp. "Haven't seen him in years, though."

"Yeah? Y'all tight back then?"

"Sort of," I replied. "We were cool, but you know how life is. People drift apart."

Big Tony said, nodding, "Still, sounds like he's looking out for you."

"Yeah. I guess he is," I added softly. Under my breath, I muttered, "I'm in too deep," hoping that the sound of the clippers would drown out what I said.

"What was that?" Bradley asked.

"Nothing," I said quickly, closing my eyes and hoping this would all be over soon.

Big Tony said with a smile in his voice. "So today's the first time y'all caught up in a minute?"

"Yeah, pretty much," I said. "I ran into him while trying to, uh, figure some stuff out."

Big Tony chuckled, pausing to adjust his clippers. "So let me get this straight. You hooked up with yo boy again after all this time to get a haircut?"

Before I could answer, Bradley chimed in from the corner with a smirk. "Man, my boy here's getting the deluxe treatment. Gotta have him lookin' sharp. For his date."

I groaned. "Can you not?"

"I'm just saying," Bradley replied, flopping onto the couch. "This is quality entertainment. Malcolm, this is exactly the kind of energy you need to bring. Nothing says 'impressive' like a kitchen fade."

Big Tony grinned. "I like this guy. He's got jokes."

"Don't encourage him," I muttered, squeezing my eyes shut as the clippers buzzed closer to my ear.

"Man, you're too uptight," Big Tony said, shaking his head. "You gotta learn to relax. Life's too short to be stressin' like this."

"Easy for you to say," I shot back. "You're not the one trying to juggle all this insanity."

Bradley leaned forward, a wicked gleam in his eye. "What insanity? You've got oxtails on the stove, a professional barber in your kitchen, and a date with a beautiful woman. Sounds like you're living the dream."

"The dream?" I repeated, incredulous. "This isn't the dream. This is a nightmare."

Big Tony let out a booming laugh. "Man, you're funny. Alright, hold still. I'm almost done."

"By the way, Big Tony. He hooked up with his home boy after all this time to score some weed," Bradley offered easily.

My eyes shot open, and I turned to glare at Bradley. "Dude!" His arms were wrapped over the back of my couch like he was reclining in a damn spa. I wanted to choke the life out of him.

The sudden movement caused Big Tony's hand to slip, and I felt a sharp buzz near my temple.

"Uhh," Big Tony said, pulling back and inspecting the damage. "I think I'm gonna have to take off a bit more than I wanted to."

"What?!" I yelped, craning my neck to try and see the mirror. Bradley, meanwhile, burst into hysterical laughter, clutching his stomach like this was the funniest thing he'd ever seen.

With no mirror in sight, I had to resign myself to letting Big Tony fix his error without me seeing the damage that had been done.

Big Tony threw his head back and laughed, the deep sound filling the room. "So that's what this is all about. My bad, man. Here I am thinkin' you just needed a fade."

I fumed, feeling like a fool.

"Relax, man," Big Tony said, still chuckling. "It ain't a big deal. You should've just said something, though. Would've saved us both some confusion."

"And time," added Bradley.

I shot Bradley a pointed look. I couldn't turn around to see Big Tony's face with him standing behind me. "I do not need commentary from the peanut gallery,"

He stepped back, studying my hair for a moment before running the clippers one last time.

As the clippers buzzed, I couldn't help but reflect on how far off course this day had gone. All I'd wanted was a simple solution, and now here I was, sitting in my own kitchen, getting roasted by Bradley and a barber I'd just met. It was surreal.

Big Tony stepped back, brushing stray hairs off my shoulders. "Alright, you're good to go. Managed to rescue it, but it's a little lower than I usually go, but you lookin' fresh, my man."

I sighed, running a hand over my head. It felt lighter than I was used to, but at least it didn't look completely botched. "Thanks," I muttered, not entirely sure if I meant it.

"No problem," Big Tony said, packing up his clippers. "So listen, about what you really need... I know a guy who can help you out."

My eyes lit up. "Seriously? That's great!"

"Yeah," he said, nodding. "But there's a catch."

I frowned. "What kind of catch?" My stomach gurgled and I got this sinking feeling.

Big Tony grinned. "You gotta go to him. He's gonna be at my barber shop later tonight. We're havin' a little dominoes game. You show up, you'll meet him."

I stared at him. "A dominoes game?" I asked, trying to process this new twist.

"Yup," he said, scribbling down an address. "Be there at six."

As he handed me the paper, I hesitated. "Thanks, I guess."

Big Tony raised an eyebrow. "Guess?"

"No, no," I said quickly. "Thank you."

He laughed, slinging his bag over his shoulder. "Oh, and one more thing..." he trailed off with his hand held out. I thought he wanted me to shake it.

"Even though it was a misunderstanding about you needing a cut, I'm still gonna have to charge you."

"Oh. Yeah, of course." I reached into my pocket, pulling out the cash I'd gotten from the ATM. "How much?

"Sixty," Big Tony said casually. "That don't include the tip."

I blinked.

"Sixty bucks? For a kitchen haircut?" I repeated, my jaw dropping.

"Yup," he said, completely unfazed. "Best in the city, man," Big Tony said with a wink. "You wanted the best, didn't you?"

Reluctantly, I handed over the cash, feeling my wallet grow remarkably lighter with the loss of just a few pieces of folded paper. As he left, Bradley's laughter echoed behind me.

Big Tony pocketed the cash with a grin and headed for the door. "See you tonight, man."

"Yeah. See ya," I managed through the shock.

"You just paid sixty bucks for a haircut you didn't even want," Bradley said, grinning from ear to ear.

I glared at him. "Not. Another. Word."

Chapter 6

As soon as Big Tony left, Bradley leaned back in his chair, arms crossed, looking entirely too pleased with himself. "Well, that was... something."

"Don't," I warned, grabbing the dish towel and returning to the sink.

"What? I'm just saying, for sixty bucks, you look like you're about to audition for a 90s boy band."

I shot him a look over my shoulder. "Are you planning to help, or are you just here for moral support?"

"I'm here for moral support."

I threw the towel at him. He picked it up and started moving into the kitchen.

Bradley smirked. "I'll help... if you admit that was the most expensive misunderstanding of your life."

"Fine. It was," I muttered, scrubbing a stubborn pan with more force than necessary. "Happy?"

"Ecstatic," Bradley said, grabbing a rag and starting to wipe down the counters. "But, in all seriousness, what's your next move? You gonna hit up this dominoes game?"

"Do I have a choice?" I asked, sighing. "If I don't show up, I'll never get what I need, and this whole day will have been a waste."

Bradley shrugged. "Could be worse. You could still not have a haircut."

I groaned, focusing on the dishes. "Remind me why we're friends again?"

"Because no one else will put up with me... I mean, you," Bradley corrected cheerfully.

Before I could respond, the doorbell rang. I tossed the towel onto the counter and turned to Bradley. "Can you get that?"

"Sure thing," Bradley said, heading to the door. I heard him greet someone, and then Tasha's voice floated in.

"Hey, Bradley. Is Malcolm here?"

"Right this way," he said, stepping aside to let her in. Her friend Renee was in tow.

Tasha walked in, carrying a small bag in one hand. Her smile brightened when she saw me. "Hey, Malcolm. I just wanted to drop this off before heading home for a bit."

"What is it?" I asked, drying my hands on my jeans as she set the bag on the counter.

"Just some dessert," she said with a shrug. "Figured it'd go well with dinner later."

She kissed me on the cheek, leaving me feeling like the luckiest guy in the world.

"That's sweet," I said, genuinely touched. "Thanks."

Just as Bradley was closing the door, the doorbell rang again. He opened it to reveal none other than my mom, Yvonne, standing there with a bright smile and a covered dish in her hands.

"Mom?" I said, my voice rising an octave. "What are you doing here?"

"I was in the neighborhood and thought I'd drop off something for you," she said innocently, stepping inside and glancing around. Her eyes landed on Tasha and Renee almost immediately. "Oh, and who are these lovely young ladies?"

Tasha turned, her smile still intact but her eyes curious. "Hi, I'm Tasha." She turned and indicated her friend, who had moved over near Bradley. "This is my friend, Renee. And you must be Malcolm's mom?"

"That's right," Yvonne said, setting the dish down on the counter and extending a hand. "Yvonne Carter. It's so nice to meet you."

Tasha shook her hand confidently. "Nice to meet you too, Mrs. Carter."

"Oh, saying it like that makes me feel old. Please, call me Yvonne," my mom said with a warm smile that I didn't entirely trust. She then turned to the other woman. "And you are?"

Renee turned to face Yvonne. Bradley had obviously gotten the girl's attention. "Renee," she said, crossing the room to shake my mother's hand in greeting. "I'm Tasha's friend. She brought me along to make sure Malcolm behaves."

Bradley let out a laugh, stepping back to take in the scene. "Oh, this just got interesting."

"It's nice to meet you Renee," my mom said, obviously ignoring Bradley. She knew how he was with me.

"Same here, Mrs..." She caught herself. "Yvonne."

I groaned internally as Yvonne sized up Renee. "Well, the more, the merrier," she said diplomatically. "So, Tasha, what do you do?"

The room felt smaller, the air heavier with unspoken expectations. I could almost hear the clock ticking as my mom's gaze locked onto Tasha, evaluating her with the precision of a drill sergeant.

I stepped between them, trying to intercept. "Mom, Tasha was just dropping something off. She's heading out soon to drop Renee off at home."

"Oh, I'm not in a rush. Are you okay with giving me some time, Renee," Tasha said, leaning against the counter.

"Sure," Renee gave in way of a reply, while waving her hand dismissively. "You only brought me along because you couldn't wait to see Malcolm as soon as possible anyway," she said, crossing her arms with a smirk.

Bradley, stepping back to take in the scene, said, "This is so good."

Renee moved back to where Bradley was. I looked at the two of them standing together, Bradley and Renee. Side by side. Too close. It made me feel uncomfortable but I couldn't figure out why. It seemed like they were finding the perfect place to watch a performance. Before I could say anything to Bradley, Tasha's voice caught my attention.

"I work just a block away, so it's easy to pop over before I head home," said Tasha to my mom, drawing my mom's attention back to her.

I shot Tasha a look, silently begging her not to encourage this. I was already worried that we'd get the fifth degree during the brunch so I wanted to brief her on what to expect from my mom and the others before then. I guess I wasn't gonna be given the chance, though.

"A block away? How convenient," Yvonne said, her tone pleasant but probing. "What kind of work do you do?"

"I'm a case manager for a non-profit," Tasha said, her voice steady but softening slightly as if she were choosing her words with care. "We help at-risk youth find housing and employment."

For a brief moment, her eyes flicked downward, a small pause that might have gone unnoticed by anyone else. When she looked back up, the warmth in her smile returned, but there was a flicker of something vulnerable in her gaze—something that made her confidence feel earned rather than effortless.

My mom's eyebrows lifted slightly, her expression softening in a way I didn't fully catch at the time. Later, I'd learn *this* was the moment she started to like Tasha—not because of her poise or charm, but because she saw someone willing to be vulnerable and strong in the same breath.

I could see her trying to process the information Tasha had given her. "That sounds... rewarding."

"It is," Tasha said simply, her calm demeanor making me simultaneously proud and nervous. As the conversation continued, she leaned back slightly, her shoulder brushing against mine. The warmth of her presence caught me off guard, cutting through the chaos of the moment like sunlight breaking through heavy clouds.

My life had always been carefully constructed—built to avoid risks and surprises. But standing there, I couldn't ignore how inadequate that structure felt against Tasha's steady confidence. She wasn't just navigating the situation; she was shaping it, turning potential tension into something almost effortless.

Her poise didn't just ground me; it challenged me to reevaluate the dull, predictable rhythm I'd always clung to. The monotony I once called safety suddenly felt hollow. Next to Tasha, even the absurdity of this day—the chaos, the unpredictability—seemed less daunting. She gave it a purpose. Or so I thought.

Without even realizing it, my hand drifted to her waist, resting there lightly as if to anchor myself. It wasn't a gesture I planned or even fully understood, but something about her presence demanded it. Maybe I just wanted to believe that her calm could extend to me, that her strength might steady my own wavering sense of control.

It was terrifying to feel so out of my depth, yet it was the most reassuring thing I'd experienced in a long time.

"You must be very busy," Yvonne said, her tone ever-so-slightly pointed.

"Sometimes," Tasha said with a shrug. "But it's important work, so I don't mind."

Bradley and Renee, who had been leaning against the wall, looked like they were watching a tennis match, their eyes darting back and forth between the my mother and Tasha. I, on the other hand, felt like I was watching a car crash in slow motion.

Renee leaned closer to Bradley and said dryly, "I think Malcolm's sweating through his shirt."

Bradley grinned. "Nah, that's just his way of blending in. It's called nervous camouflage."

"I mean, I could've handled Malcolm's mom just as well as Tasha," Bradley added with a smirk.

Renee quipped, "Sure, if handling involves hiding in the kitchen and letting the pros take over."

I clenched my jaw and shot them both a warning look. "Are you two practicing a comedy routine, or is this just a special performance for me?"

They ignored me completely, grinning like Cheshire cats.

"Mom," I said, trying to redirect. "Thanks for the..." I trailed off. I didn't know what she had brought. "What is this?" I asked.

"It's your favorite dessert for your dinner, dear," my mom said pleasantly.

I looked back at the kitchen counter. To the dish that Tasha had just brought but I said nothing about it.

Turning back to my mom, I kept talking. "Thanks for the dessert, but Tasha really does have to go. You wanna get home soon, right Renee? Long day and all."

Renee seemed like she didn't hear me. She instantly found her fingernails intriguing and glanced at them intently as they need her immediate scrutiny.

"Oh, it's no trouble," Tasha said, ignoring me completely. "I actually wanted to ask you something, Yvonne."

My stomach dropped. "Tasha..."

"What's that?" my mom asked, her curiosity piqued.

"Do you have any embarrassing baby pictures of Malcolm?" Tasha asked, her eyes sparkling with mischief.

Bradley and Renee let out a bark of laughter.

Bradley said with a knowing grin, "I gotta hand it to her—mentioning baby pictures? That's like waving a magic wand. Nobody can resist baby pictures."

Renee added, her tone dry and amused, "Especially the embarrassing ones. They're like kryptonite for dignity."

Bradley said, his grin widening as though he'd uncovered a universal truth. "That's like a cheat code for moms. Everyone loves 'em."

Renee, smirking, added with dry amusement, "Especially the ones that look like a Hall of Fame for bad decisions."

I groaned loudly, running my hand down my face. This motion alone reminded me that I was quick to becoming a running joke soon.

My mom, on the other hand, widened her smile. "Do I? Honey, I have albums."

"Great," Tasha said, grinning at me. "I'd love to see them sometime."

I groaned, pinching the bridge of my nose. "I need a drink."

"Don't worry," Renee said, patting me on the shoulder. "This is way more entertaining."

"She's right," Bradley added. "This is peak family bonding."

Bradley walked off in direction of the kitchen, waiting at the opening and shaking his head. I could have sworn that his shoulders were shaking too, as he suppressed a laugh.

I turned to Tasha, hoping to salvage what was left of my sanity. "Hey, just so you know, dinner's going to be a little late. I've got somewhere I need to be by six. Would seven thirty, maybe eight work for you? I know it's a little late."

Tasha, barely registering what I'd said, waved me off with a smile. "That's fine. No rush."

"Okay, I'll send you a text letting you know when I'm back from that errand and..." I began.

Before I could say anything else, my mom, clearly delighted to have met Tasha, looped her arm through Tasha's and started leading her toward the door. "Come on, Tasha. Let me tell you about the time Malcolm tried to roller skate in the living room."

"Oh, I've got to hear this," Tasha said, laughing as she let herself be guided out of the apartment.

Renee shook her head, smirking. "Guess I'll ride along for that story."

I stood frozen, watching the three of them leave, my mom happily chattering away about my childhood. Bradley leaned against the counter, looking as smug as ever.

"What just happened?" I muttered, mostly to myself. I hadn't expected my mom to warm up to Tasha so quickly, and I couldn't help but wonder if it was because of that question about baby pictures. Knowing my mom, the mere mention of her "baby boy" was enough to win her over completely.

As if to confirm my thoughts, I could still hear her voice in the hallway, cheerfully recounting another embarrassing story as the door clicked shut behind them.

Bradley shook his head, grinning. "Your mom just got played like a fiddle."

I groaned loudly, burying my face in my hands. "Don't start."

"Too late," he said, laughing. "You've got yourself a keeper, Malcolm. And apparently, she's already got your mom wrapped around her finger."

"I'm doomed," I muttered, heading back to the sink to finish cleaning. But deep down, I couldn't help but smile a little.

Chapter 7

As I finished wiping down the last of the counters, my phone buzzed on the table. I grabbed it, glancing at the screen. Darius.

"Yo, Malcolm!" Darius's voice came through the speaker, loud and full of energy. "Man, I'm done with work. Only had to put in a couple of hours today—flexible schedule perks."

"Must be nice," I said, trying to sound casual as I threw the dish towel over my shoulder.

"So, Big Tony get in touch with you?"

I sighed. "Yeah, he did."

Before I could elaborate, Bradley, who had taken up residence on my couch, chimed in. "Oh, you mean Big Tony? The guy Malcolm thought was pulling out a gun but was actually pulling out clippers?"

"Dude!" I snapped, glaring at him. "That was not what happened."

"It totally was," Bradley said, grinning. "The look on your face was priceless."

Darius burst out laughing. "Wait, wait, hold up. You thought Big Tony was gonna shoot you?"

"No," I said firmly. "I was just... caught off guard."

"Man, you're something else," Darius said between laughs. "Alright, so what's the deal? What's Tony got you doing?"

I filled him in on the dominoes game and the promise of meeting someone who could finally help me out. As I talked, Bradley kept adding his two cents, much to my irritation.

"You should've seen him when Tony started talking about setting up for a haircut," Bradley said. "Malcolm looked like he'd never heard of clippers before."

"Okay, we've established I misunderstood," I said through gritted teeth. "Can we move on?"

"Man, I'm dying over here," Darius said, still laughing. "Alright, alright. I'll meet y'all at Tony's barber shop later. We'll get this handled."

"Fine," I muttered, already dreading whatever else the night had in store.

"Cool. See you then," Darius said before hanging up.

I tossed my phone onto the counter and turned to Bradley. "You just had to share all that, didn't you?"

"Absolutely," Bradley said, smirking. "What are friends for?"

I groaned, rubbing my temples. "This night better go smoothly. That's all I'm saying."

"Define smoothly," Bradley said with a laugh as he leaned back on the couch. "Because I have a feeling we're about to redefine it."

By the time Bradley and I arrived at Big Tony's barber shop, the sun had dipped below the horizon, and the place was buzzing with energy. The sound of dominoes clattering against a table echoed out onto the sidewalk as we stepped inside. The shop had been transformed into a makeshift gaming hall, with chairs and tables rearranged to accommodate the crowd. A dozen people milled around, laughing, shouting, and cheering at the action.

Big Tony greeted us with a wide grin and a nod toward the dominoes table. "Malcolm, Bradley, glad y'all made it. Reggie's already here."

My stomach churned as I followed his gesture to the table, where three men were seated, their faces a mix of concentration and amusement. Reggie, a wiry man with sharp features and an easy smile, gave me a wave as I approached.

"Malcolm, right?" Reggie said, gesturing to the empty seat beside him. "Come on, we saved you a spot."

"Uh, sure," I said, sliding into the chair. As I settled in, Reggie slid a fresh stack of dominoes toward me. "Draw your hand."

I hesitated, looking around at the expectant faces. Bradley, ever the wildcard, pulled up a chair on my other side after that man declared that he was out. He grabbed his own set of dominoes, earning surprised looks from the regulars.

"Bradley?" I asked, incredulous.

"What? I've played before," he said with a shrug. "Can't let you have all the fun."

Reggie smirked. "Alright, looks like we've got a full table. Let's get started."

As I drew my tiles, the rules were quickly laid out. Each hand required a $5 buy-in, and losers paid $1 for every five points they lost by in that hand. The game would go to 350 points, which meant the stakes could escalate fast. My stomach tightened as I did the math—if someone scored nothing by the end of the game, they'd owe $75. That didn't count the tally at the end of each hand. Even getting your name on the score card required earning at least fifteen points and that didn't count towards the goal of 350 points, a sobering reminder of how easy it was to end up with a big fat zero.

"High-stakes dominoes," Bradley whispered, barely containing his excitement. "This is awesome."

"That's one word for it," I muttered, already second-guessing my decision to sit down.

The game kicked off, and I immediately felt out of my depth. The other players slammed their tiles onto the table with gusto, calling out points with practiced ease. I, on the other hand, hesitated with every move, overthinking every possible outcome. The tension in my chest grew with each hand as I tried to focus on the game while simultaneously wondering how I was supposed to broach the subject of weed with Reggie.

Reggie, however, seemed completely unbothered. After a particularly decisive win, he leaned back in his chair and flashed me a grin. "Don't sweat it, man. We'll handle that business after a few hands."

His casual attitude did little to calm my nerves, but at least I knew the topic was on the table—just not this table.

Bradley, meanwhile, was thriving. To my astonishment, he played with a confidence and flair that earned him nods of approval from the other players. He slammed down tiles with gusto, his trash talk earning laughs from the crowd.

"Gimme that twenny-twen-twen!" he shouted after one particularly bold move, collecting his winnings with a triumphant grin. The room erupted in laughter, and for a moment, I forgot my own nerves.

The crowd around us grew louder as the game progressed. Each hand brought new highs and lows, with money exchanging hands at a dizzying pace. My pile of chips fluctuated wildly, and I couldn't help but feel like I was barely holding on.

"You good, Malcolm?" Reggie asked after one round where I'd barely escaped losing big.

"Yeah," I said quickly, though my voice wavered. "Just... not used to this kind of game."

Reggie chuckled. "You'll get the hang of it. Just don't overthink it."

Easy for him to say. The man played like he had dominoes in his DNA. Meanwhile, I felt like I was walking a tightrope with no safety net.

Bradley, of course, was having the time of his life. "This is way better than Monopoly," he said, slapping another tile onto the table. "And you don't have to mortgage your house to keep playing."

I groaned. "Speak for yourself. I think I'm losing my rent money over here."

The group laughed, and even I couldn't help but crack a small smile. Despite my nerves, there was something oddly exhilarating about the chaos of the game. Still, I couldn't shake the nagging feeling that I was in over my head. And with the weight of the evening's real objective hanging over me, I knew the night was far from over.

By the end of the game, I was down seventy-five dollars. It stung, but considering how high the stakes had been, I knew it could've been much worse. As I pushed back my chair, Reggie gestured for me to follow him. "Come on, man, let's step away from the table."

Bradley remained behind, laughing and bantering with the other players like he'd been part of their circle for years. I envied his ability to blend in so effortlessly.

Reggie led me to a quieter corner of the shop, away from the dominoes table. As we settled, I finally got a good look at him. He was clean-cut, wearing neatly pressed slacks and a button-down shirt, and didn't look much older than me. For some reason, I'd expected someone... different. Less polished, maybe?

"You look surprised," Reggie said, catching my expression.

I cleared my throat. "No, no. I just... you're not what I expected."

Reggie chuckled, shaking his head. "Let me guess. You thought I'd be rocking baggy clothes and gold chains?"

"I mean...," I stammered, embarrassed. "Not exactly."

"It's cool," he said, leaning back against the wall. "You're not the first to make that assumption. But nah, man. This is just temporary."

"Temporary?" I asked, my curiosity piqued.

"Yeah," Reggie said, his tone more serious now. "I'm saving up to go legit."

"Legit?"

"I went to UGA," he said casually, like it was no big deal. "Got a degree in botany. My whole setup is in my basement—greenhouse and all. I'm just selling weed right now to save up the cash to get licensed as a legal grower."

I blinked, trying to reconcile the image in front of me with the stereotypical idea I'd had in my head. "Wait... so you're... what? A startup?"

Reggie laughed. "You could say that. Darius and Big Tony are already partners in the business. Within a month or so, we should be fully licensed, certified, and legal."

I nodded slowly, letting that sink in. "So, all of this... it's just a stepping stone."

"Exactly," Reggie said, his expression proud. "It's not just about the money, though. It's about doing something I actually care about. Growing is an art, man. And once we're legal, we can do it the right way—no cutting corners, no middlemen. Just good product, done right."

"That's impressive," I admitted.

"Appreciate it," Reggie said, giving me a small nod. "So, you ready to take care of business?"

I hesitated for a moment before nodding. "Yeah. Let's do this." We wrapped up the transaction quickly and discreetly. For the first time in what felt like forever, I held the little bag in my hand and felt a wave of relief. After all the hoops I'd jumped through, I couldn't help but wonder: was this really all it took? All that stress for this?

For the first time that evening, I felt a little less uneasy. Reggie wasn't just some dealer trying to make a quick buck. He had a plan, a vision, and he was working toward it with determination.

As Reggie and I walked back to the table, the crowd seemed even larger than before. The atmosphere was electric, with everyone's attention focused on Bradley, who was still sitting at the dominoes table. My jaw nearly dropped when I saw the stack of cash in front of him.

"What's going on?" I asked Reggie, nodding toward the table.

"Looks like your boy's been cleaning house," Reggie said with a grin. "He's good."

I took a seat a few steps back, choosing to observe rather than join the chaos. Bradley looked entirely too smug, his cocky grin growing wider with each play. The girl sitting opposite him, though, was the real puzzle. She was practically draped over the table, leaning in way too close for someone who was just a casual spectator.

"Malcolm!" Bradley called, spotting me. "You're just in time. Meet Tasha."

I blinked. "Tasha?"

The girl waved, her eyes flickering briefly in my direction before locking back onto Bradley. "Nice to meet you, Malcolm," she said smoothly.

Of course. Of course, her name was Tasha. Because... why wouldn't it be?

As Bradley played, she leaned in closer, her perfectly glossed lips curving into a calculated smile. The subtle tilt of her head as she whispered something to him—it was all too familiar. I'd seen this playbook before. Late-night binges of Catfish had shown me how this script went. Step one: charm the mark. Step two: inflate their ego just enough to make them think they're in control. Step three: profit.

Bradley basked in the glow of his winning streak, slamming down tiles with a flourish and scoring big while the crowd erupted in cheers. Meanwhile, New Tasha leaned in, her laughter lingering just a little too long, her hand casually resting on his arm like she'd done it a hundred times before.

"You better watch yourself, Bradley," one of the players teased. "Tasha's got that look in her eye."

Without Bradley noticing, she flipped the guy the finger. She mouthed to him to shut the f— up. I saw it even though she was trying to be covert. The way her hand lingered on his arm, her laugh just a little too practiced—it all felt like watching a magician setting up a trick.

"Man, Bradley's got Tasha sitting close? That girl doesn't lean in for free," one of the other players muttered, shaking his head with a grin.

Bradley waved him off, grinning like he was untouchable. But I noticed the way her smile didn't quite reach her eyes, the way every move she made seemed curated to keep him hooked. She's playing him, I thought, the realization clicking into place. And Bradley? He didn't even see it coming.

Bradley was in his element, talking smack like he was born to do it. "You ain't ready for this heat. Give me two-tens!" he declared, slamming down a tile with a flourish and neatly scoring twenty points. The crowd around the table erupted in laughter and cheers, clearly entertained by his antics.

On his next turn, he glanced slyly at the player to his left and shook his head, a smug grin spreading across his face. "Next!" he shouted as he slammed down a tile, his voice cutting through the noise as his opponent grumbled and muttered about not being able to play. The onlookers howled with laughter, clapping and shouting encouragement.

Even I had to admit, I was impressed. "Bradley," I asked, curiosity getting the better of me, "how did you get so good at this?"

My question came out louder than I intended, and suddenly all eyes were on him. The room fell quiet, everyone waiting for his answer.

Bradley leaned back in his chair, a self-satisfied grin on his face. "I went to Morehouse College," he said, the words landing like a bombshell.

The silence was deafening for a moment before someone blurted out, "Wait, what?"

"Yeah," Bradley continued, seemingly unfazed by the stunned reactions. "I started at Morehouse. Wanted to get a degree in medicine, but it didn't work out."

"Didn't work out?" I asked, frowning. This was news to me.

Bradley nodded, his tone turning more reflective. "Yeah. I thought I wanted to be a doctor, but the other side of it just wasn't for me. Sitting with patients' families while they held vigils for the terminally ill, dealing with bedpans, seeing the indignity some patients faced in their final moments... I couldn't handle it."

The crowd was quiet now, listening intently. Even the new Tasha seemed captivated.

"So, I transferred to Clark Atlanta," Bradley continued. "Switched to a business degree, and that's where I met Malcolm." He gestured toward me with a casual wave.

I blinked, trying to process everything he'd just said. I'd known Bradley had transferred from Morehouse in his junior year, but I'd never heard the full story before. It was strange, realizing there was so much about my best friend that I didn't know.

"Man," Reggie said, breaking the silence. "Respect. That's a heavy choice."

Bradley shrugged, his easygoing smile back in place. "Life's about figuring out what you can handle and what you can't, right?"

It wasn't just about the studying medicine at a historically black college. It was also about his race.

"Morehouse taught me a lot," Bradley said, his usual grin softening. "But not all lessons are in the classroom. Sometimes you learn what you can't handle, and that's just as important."

The crowd murmured their agreement, and just like that, the tension broke. The game resumed, but I couldn't shake the feeling that I'd just seen a side of Bradley I hadn't known existed. As he played another bold move and collected his winnings with a triumphant grin, I couldn't help but think that there was a lot more to him than met the eye.

The game wrapped up, and to my surprise, Bradley didn't just win—he dominated. With nearly $700 in winnings, he finally stood, his grin as smug as ever. But what caught my eye was the new Tasha, who seemed glued to his side.

Bradley grabbed his cash and stretched. "Well, fellas, that was fun."

The crowd dispersed slightly, giving him congratulatory slaps on the back or nods of approval. While Bradley was over there living it up, It was then that Darius appeared at my side, nodding toward Bradley and the New Tasha. "Yo, Malcolm, you might wanna get your boy. Unless you want him to become the new 'Captain Save a Hoe.'"

I frowned, "Tasha?" I looked back at Bradley, having stupidly thought he'd let her slide away when he got ready to leave. I was wrong.

She stood a bit away from him but still close enough to stake a claim. She watched him as he talked to those that had gathered around him.

Her eyes lingering on Bradley like a predator sizing up its next meal. Bradley, of course, was oblivious, laughing about his winnings and already counting how many drinks he could buy with the cash. I knew I should say something, warn him again, but what was the point? Bradley wasn't the type to listen—not until it hit him where it hurt.

Still, I couldn't shake the feeling that if I didn't step in now, tonight was just the beginning. For all his confidence, Bradley was stepping into a game he didn't even realize he was playing. And the worst part? I had a front-row seat.

Darius smirked. "That girl? She's got game, man. She'll stick around just long enough to milk him dry. You know... get her nails done, hair done, all on him, and then bounce."

I groaned, running a hand down my face. "Of course."

Darius clapped me on the shoulder. "Better grab him now."

I glanced back at Bradley, who was laughing at something New Tasha said. For a guy who didn't seem to have much experience with urban culture, he sure fit right in. Still, he didn't know it all. Sighing, I walked over and nudged him on the arm.

"Hey, Bradley," I said, keeping my tone light. "We should probably head out."

"What? Already?" he asked, looking genuinely disappointed.

New Tasha gave me a side-eye but didn't say anything.

"Yeah," I said firmly. "We've got a long day tomorrow."

Bradley raised an eyebrow but shrugged. "Alright, man, your call."

As we left the shop, I glanced over my shoulder to see new Tasha watching us go, her expression unreadable. Bradley, oblivious as ever, was already counting his winnings.

"Darius said that girl's bad news," I told Bradley.

He looked over his shoulder at New Tasha. She was standing in the door as we stood on the sidewalk. "Her? Naw, she's cool. I like her vibe."

"Darius isn't wrong," I said, cutting Bradley off before he could dismiss it. "Girls like her? They know exactly what they're doing. First, it's all smiles and compliments. Then, it's a casual 'Can you cover this bill?' Next thing you know, she's got her nails done, her hair done, and you're wondering where your paycheck went."

Bradley blinked at me, clearly surprised. "Where'd you even get that idea, man?"

I shrugged. "You ever watch Catfish? Same story, different setting. Just—don't be stupid, okay?"

"Yeah," he sighed regrettably. "I guess you're right. It did seem too good to be true."

"Well I'm glad you're listening to me, buddy."

We turned and continued to walk back to the car.

"Man, this was a great night," he said cheerfully.

I groaned. "You're impossible."

He laughed, slapping me on the back. "What are friends for?"

I rolled my eyes, but a thought struck me. "Well, if we're such good friends, how about you hook me up with sixty bucks from those winnings so I can at least recoup the cost of my haircut?"

Bradley stopped walking and stared at me blankly. For a split second, I thought he might actually consider it. Then, he threw his head back and laughed so hard he nearly doubled over.

"Sixty bucks? Man, you're hilarious!" he said, wiping a tear from the corner of his eye. "But don't worry, I got you covered."

I narrowed my eyes at him. "Covered how?"

"You'll see," he said with a grin that made me instantly regret asking. "Just trust me."

I sighed, shaking my head. "Every time you say that, I end up regretting it."

"Oh, come on," Bradley said, slinging an arm around my shoulder. "You've survived this far. What's the worst that could happen?"

Chapter 8

By the time I got home, I was running on fumes. Bradley had finally gone his own way after we stopped by my apartment to grab his car. To my surprise, he'd handed me sixty bucks for the haircut—and another hundred to make up for what I'd lost at the dominoes game.

"Consider it a sponsorship," he'd said with a wink. "You're my entertainment for the night, after all."

I didn't have the energy to argue, and I wasn't about to turn down free money. Still, I couldn't help but mutter, "You're impossible," as he sauntered off.

When I stepped back into my apartment, a sharp, charred smell hit my nose. My heart sank.

"No, no, no," I muttered, rushing into the kitchen. The pot on the stove was hissing and spitting, half the liquid gone. The oxtails, which I'd left on a low simmer, were now well into the realm of overcooked.

"You've got to be kidding me," I groaned, grabbing a spoon to inspect the damage. The meat looked dry, and the sauce was almost reduced to nothing.

I scrambled to add more broth, stirring frantically while trying to salvage what I could. "This was supposed to be simple! Just a nice dinner! How did it turn into... this?"

The doorbell rang, jolting me out of my panic. My heart skipped a beat. Tasha. She wasn't supposed to be here yet.

Wiping my hands on a dish towel, I hurried to the door, trying to ignore the chaos behind me. I opened it to find her standing there, a bright smile on her face.

"Hey," she said, holding up a small bag. "I brought wine."

"Hey," I said, my voice a little higher-pitched than I intended. "You're early."

She shrugged. "I figured I'd stop by since I've already dropped Renee off and been home to check on my mom. Is that okay? I didn't feel like waiting for your text to tell let me know to come over."

Her eyes held a plea I couldn't ignore. Damn puppy-dog eyes. Nature really knew what it was doing with babies, puppies, and kittens—the way their eyes shimmered with a silent, heart-wrenching cry for something. It was downright brutal.

"Uh, yeah, of course," I said, stepping aside to let her in. My eyes darted to the kitchen, where the pot was still bubbling ominously on the stove.

Tasha walked in and set the bag on the counter, her eyes scanning the room. "Did you have trouble making dinner?" she asked, her nose upturned. "You didn't have to go all out."

I forced a laugh. "You know me. Always aiming to impress."

Her gaze lingered on the pot, and I held my breath. "What's still... cooking?"

"Oxtails," I said, trying to sound casual. "They're, uh, almost done," I lied.

"Smells... interesting," she said, turning towards me and raising an eyebrow.

I cleared my throat. "Dinner might be a little late. I... lost track of time while I was out. I left it to simmer, I thought." I looked into the pot before I turned back to her and said, "I thought I wouldn't be gone that long so now I think I ruined the meal."

"That's fine," she said, waving me off. "If you want, we can do something else then."

She pulled out her phone without further comment, and I slumped against the counter, staring at the pot like it had personally betrayed me. With the added broth, the oxtails didn't look completely ruined, but they weren't going to win any culinary awards either.

Seeing my defeated look, Tasha paused in her scrolling and moved further into the kitchen where she could inspect the mess I'd made. She took a spoon and dipped some of the sauce into it to taste it. "It's not totally ruined. Let's put on some rice to go with it."

I gave her another look that she immediately understood.

"You don't have any rice, do you?" she asked.

I shook my head.

"I'll pop out to the store to get some. You see what you can do with the oxtails," she offered.

By the time I got everything cleaned up and the table set, the doorbell rang again. This time, Tasha was back, grocery bag in hand.

"Smells better now," she said, stepping inside and glancing around.

"I did what I could," I admitted, trying not to sound too defeated.

After cleaning up the kitchen a bit more, Tasha leaned against the counter, watching me fumble with the last of the dishes, putting them through the dishwasher while we ate. "Relax, Malcolm. It's just dinner," she said, her voice teasing. "You're not auditioning for Top Chef."

"You say that now," I muttered, wiping my hands. "But you haven't tasted the oxtails."

She laughed, shaking her head. "I've got a feeling they'll be fine."

Dinner was... fine. The clink of forks against plates filled the silence as we ate, the occasional scrape of my chair against the tile floor the only other sound. Tasha sat across from me, her posture relaxed as she took small, deliberate bites. Her face gave nothing away—not a grimace, not a wince, but not exactly a glowing review either.

I watched her out of the corner of my eye, trying to gauge her reaction. She didn't hesitate to take a second bite, but there was no sparkle of delight, no quick comment about how good it was. The oxtails looked passable, their glossy sauce glinting under the warm kitchen light, but every chew felt like a countdown to her saying, You tried.

"So, uh," I started, my fork hesitating mid-air, "how's the sauce?"

Tasha looked up, a faint smile on her lips. "It's good," she said simply, before taking another bite.

Good? That could mean anything. "Not too salty?" I asked, my voice straining to sound casual.

She shook her head. "No, it's fine."

Fine. The least reassuring word in the world. I shifted in my seat, poking at my food as my thoughts raced. She wasn't lying—there was no hint of distaste in her expression—but there wasn't much else either. No satisfied sigh, no casual compliment about the flavor. Just polite neutrality.

The quiet stretched on, punctuated only by the faint hum of the fridge and the occasional clatter of her fork against the plate. My own bites tasted bland, each one heavier than the last. The meal wasn't terrible, but it wasn't the kind of dinner that left you lingering over the table, savoring every morsel.

When she finally set her fork down, she glanced up at me and smiled again, this time a little wider. "The sauce is nice," she said. "Really."

"Thanks," I murmured, though her words felt more like a courtesy than encouragement. Still, I couldn't help but feel a small weight lift. At least she wasn't running for the door.

Tasha leaned back in her chair, brushing her fingers lightly over the rim of her wine glass. "Sometimes it's not about how perfect the meal is," she said, her voice soft. "It's about the company."

I managed a faint smile in return, grateful for her kindness even if I didn't believe her completely. As I cleared the plates, the silence felt a little less daunting—but only just.

"However," she began, and my stomach tightened.

"I actually do like how the meat falls right off the bone. Most times, you have to use your hands to eat oxtails if you want to get all the meat," she said, smiling honestly.

It wasn't a glowing review, but it was reassuring. For the first time that evening, I felt a flicker of pride—at least she appreciated the effort.

After clearing the plates and tidying up, I heard Tasha call out from the living room. "Malcolm, do you mind if I borrow one of your shirts? I spilled a little on mine."

"Uh, yeah," I called back. "Top drawer in the bedroom."

A few minutes later, I finished wiping down the counter and headed toward the couch. When I saw her, I stopped in my tracks. Tasha was curled up, wearing one of my button-down shirts—nothing else—and grinning at me like she'd been waiting for my reaction.

"Comfortable?" I asked, trying to sound casual, even as my heart raced.

"Very," she said, patting the spot beside her. "You should join me."

I couldn't help but chuckle as I took a seat. She looked so at ease, like she belonged here, and I couldn't deny how much I liked seeing her like that.

I settled on the couch where she gestured, trying to play it cool, but the awkwardness hit almost immediately. My thoughts raced, my body unsure of where to rest, and I realized I hadn't planned for the night to stretch this far. The idea of her possibly staying over kept looping in my head like a song stuck on repeat, impossible to shake. Glancing at her in my shirt only confirmed that playback couldn't be ignored.

"So," she said after a while, leaning back in her chair, "I've been meaning to talk to you about something."

I tensed slightly, unsure of where this was going. "What's up?"

She hesitated for a moment, biting her lip. "I really like you, Malcolm."

I blinked. "I like you too."

"No, I mean..." She trailed off, her gaze dropping to her hands before looking back at me. "I've dated some... not-so-great guys in the past. But with you, it's different. You're thoughtful, kind, and you actually care. That's rare."

My chest tightened. "Thanks. That means a lot."

She smiled, but it didn't quite reach her eyes. "I just wanted to say that... I hope this works out. I want this to last."

"I do too," I said, my voice soft but firm. "I mean, I really do."

Her shoulders relaxed, and her smile brightened. "Good. Because I've been thinking about the future."

"Future?" I echoed, feeling a mix of excitement and nervousness.

"Not right away," she said quickly, holding up her hands. "But maybe, down the line, we could... move in together."

"Move in together?" My brain felt like it short-circuited, half of me wanting to blurt out "Let's do it now" while the other half panicked at the thought of sharing a closet. I nodded, swallowing hard to keep my voice steady. "I'd like that. When the time is right."

She reached across the negligible space between us and took my hand, giving it a gentle squeeze. "You're a good guy, Malcolm. I'm lucky to have you."

"I think I'm the lucky one," I said, my earlier stress melting away. For a moment, I let her words settle, but the quiet between us grew heavy in my mind. Scrambling for something to do, I grabbed the remote. "How about a flick?" I suggested, aiming for casual but feeling anything but.

She laughed softly, her understanding smile making me wonder if she could see right through me. "Sure," she replied.

We settled in to watch something—I couldn't tell you what. My mind wasn't on the screen. It was on the way she shifted closer, the scent of her perfume mingling with the fabric of my shirt, the warmth of her presence. By the time the credits rolled, I hadn't absorbed a single scene.

Clearing my throat, I mustered the courage to say what had been on my mind. "I was thinking, maybe, we could... you know, relax a little." I was thinking the time was just right. Maybe this would help me seem less uptight. Everyone smoked, right? At least, that's what the movies made it seem like.

Tasha raised an eyebrow. "Relax?"

"Yeah, like, uh... maybe smoke a little weed?" I said, trying to sound nonchalant.

She stared at me for a moment before bursting into laughter. "You? Smoke weed?"

"Why not?" I said, feeling a bit defensive. "I went through a lot to get it, you know."

"Wait, you actually got some?" she asked, her eyes wide with amusement.

I nodded, pulling out the small bag like it was some kind of trophy. "Ta-da."

Tasha shook her head, still laughing. "Malcolm, I don't smoke."

"You don't... what?" I stared at her, dumbfounded. "Then why did I—"

"I don't know!" she said, giggling. "You're the one who decided this was a good idea."

I slumped back on the couch, running a hand over my face. "Unbelievable." Of course. The one time I try to look cool and spontaneous, it backfires completely.

Tasha reached across the space, her laughter softening into a smile. "Hey, I appreciate the effort. Really."

I looked up at her, still trying to process everything. I watched as she slowly stood up. She leaned over me and whispered in my ear.

"You know," she said, her tone playful, "this fits me better than you." Tasha tilted her head, her smile widening as she tugged at the hem of my shirt.

"Debatable," I shot back, trying to mask my nervousness.

She stepped closer, her hand brushing mine. "Care to prove me wrong?"

When she took a step back and slipped off her panties without revealing anything in the process, leaving only my oversized button-down shirt, I gave up trying to think. Her movements were deliberate, confident, leaving me no room to over process. She held out her hand, her smile turning mischievous.

She winked. "Come on," she said, her voice low.

I didn't need to be told twice. Taking her hand, I let her lead me to the bedroom, the absurdity of the day fading into the background.

Chapter 9

Bradley and I were sitting at his desk. He'd called me over as soon as he saw me entering the floor. He waved over, calling loudly, to my embarrassment. Most of the morning crowd had already settled at their work stations, and upon hearing someone call like that, their eyes would automatically scan to see who was being called.

I leaned back in the chair, while Bradley sat down his cup. I knew he was about to ask how the rest of the night went when I saw that damn smirk on his face.

"So," he drawled out, in true southern fashion, accent and all, "how'd the rest of the night go with Tasha?"

"Unlike the night you might have had with New Tasha, my night turned out great," I grinned.

Bradley visibly shuddered. I was sure he recalled what might have happened to him if I hadn't stepped in to guide him away from New Tasha. He would have become her new sugar daddy and 'Captain Save-a-Hoe' all wrapped up in one nice package.

I got my jab in. A cheetah couldn't have smiled more sinisterly while looking at a nice fat new born gazelle than I did. I leaned back and kicked my feet up on his desk and threw my hands behind my head. It was my turn to be smug.

He raised an eyebrow. "No problem with the weed?" he asked casually, the smile never fading from his eyes, they sparkled with mischief.

"Um," I stammered as my feet slipped off his desk and onto the floor. He'd caught me off guard. I hadn't wanted to discuss that particular event. I still felt like a fool from seeing Tasha's reaction. My head hung to my lap as I leaned forward, trying to hasten my escape and leave before revealing the flop it was. "I gotta get back to my desk. Gotta get ready to get those reports done."

I hand't even so much as straightened up when he delivered a blow that left me resuming my seat, dropping heavily like a sack of wheat.

"You really thought mugwort tea was street slang? Man, you're like a Hallmark card wrapped in a tax form," Bradley quipped.

"Well, you were no help," I retorted. "Getting something from you in the way of help was like rubbing two ice cubes together expecting to get fire." I was done with being the butt off his jokes. It was too early in the morning. Too much other crap that would end up leaving me exhausted mentally than dealing with his jokes.

He chuckled, clearly enjoying himself. "Come on, Malcolm. I'm just saying, it's a little funny."

I sighed heavily, running a hand down my face. It was too early for this. I tried to get up to leave again and he restrained me with a hand. He leaned over conspiratorially and stared into my eyes. It seemed like I was looking into the eyes of a tiger and I was just a bunny unfortunately caught in his sights.

"You know," Bradley said, sipping his coffee, "that whole escapade yesterday felt like when my brother said he couldn't find a good mechanic for his car. Hell of a time he had trying to find one. He loves that damn car. Classic '58 Buick."

I waited. I was too smart to ask.

Bradley, acting like the silence never happened, said "And then..."

Again with the frustrating pause. I waited, not daring to be baited.

"He remembered our neighbor owns a repair shop."

Something didn't feel right. I frowned, thinking this was going to be something I didn't want to ask but the problem was... I wanted to ask about it. I just did. I had a morbid curiosity that seriously nagged me to ask him to explain that statement.

Without realizing I'd done it, I asked softly, "what the hell does that mean?" I should have known better than to indulge my curiosity.

"You know, I reminded him after he asked me," Bradley said, leaning back with a satisfied grin. "You really should've just asked me first."

I blinked at him. "What?"

"Yeah," Bradley continued, completely nonchalant. "My brother sells the stuff. Like, for real. He's got the whole setup—labels, everything. He even does delivery. You could've saved yourself all this trouble if you'd asked me if I 'know a guy.'"

I stared at him, my mouth hanging open. "You're telling me I went through all of this—this—because you forgot to mention that your brother sells weed?"

Bradley shrugged, looking more amused than guilty. "Well, you never asked." He paused for dramatic effect, then added with a wink, "Guess you knew a guy after all, huh?"

"The whole time, I thought I was breaking new ground, 'expanding my horizons,' when really, I could've just sent a text. Turns out, I did 'know a guy who knew a guy.' And that guy was Bradley, of all people. Go figure," I whispered.

Bradley slowly took a sip from that damn coffee cup. He didn't even blink.

"Ten minutes," I repeated, staring at him in shock. "You're telling me I spent an entire day humiliating myself—health food stores, sketchy parking lots, mugwort tea—and your brother could've just... handed it to me?" I stared at him, dumbfounded.

Bradley shrugged. "Well, yeah. But you never asked."

I would have said something but he was too damn fast.

"Can't believe you really thought mugwort tea was slang for weed?" he laughed under his breath quickly.

I shot him an evil glance. "Stuff it! I didn't know I had to ask!" I said, my voice rising. "Why wouldn't you just say something?"

Bradley grinned. "Because."

Simple. Easy. Succint. My hands shook. I wanted to choke him.

"Watching you figure it out was way more entertaining," he finished.

I groaned, burying my face in my hands. "I can't believe this."

Bradley chuckled, leaning forward. "Hey, look at it this way. You thought you didn't know a guy. Turns out, you did. You knew me, and I knew a guy."

I glared at him from between my fingers. "Not. Helping," I hissed through gritted teeth.

Bradley raised his coffee cup like he was toasting to my misery. "Cheers, buddy. Glad I could bring some clarity to your life."

Then, because he couldn't resist, he delivered one last jab. I guess a nice rib shot to go with the gut punch that followed the preceding sucker punch. "So was it worth it?" he asked straight faced.

I stared at him, long and hard, willing him to combust under my gaze. "Was it worth it?" I echoed, my voice dangerously calm. He asks if it was worth the disaster I'd made it out to be to get to find a weed man. I had to think. I made up my mind and smiled at him, calmer now than I'd been this whole time, after taking an honest look at what I'd done. "Naw man, If I had to say. It wasn't even worth the bother. But it was fun."

I punched him in the arm—not gently—and sauntered toward my desk a few feet away. Just as I turned, I called over my shoulder, "I should report you to HR for harassment, you know."

Bradley laughed, picking up another coffee cup from the desk. "Here, I got you one too," he said, offering me the other cardboard tube of goodness. It was our usual ritual—coffee, with just the right amount of creamer.

I took the cup with a humph... and a smile. "I should still report your ass."

"You'd never," he shot back, his grin smug as ever.

The thought crossed my mind to do it just to knock him down a peg. Maybe report him for leaving wrappers in the canteen. But as I walked away, I realized I wasn't even mad anymore.

"Maybe I needed to make a fool of myself to realize how much I overthink everything," I called over my shoulder. "Or maybe I just needed a laugh. Either way, I'm not mad about it anymore."

Bradley's laugh followed me to my desk, a sound both infuriating and oddly comforting.

explicitus est liber

Also by J. A. Springs

Chronicles of Cosmic Realms
Shadows of the Forgotten Void

elctrcsheepdrmwrks (Electric Sheep Dreamworks)
Blurred Vision
Fractured
Zero One

Essays in Systems and Being
Essays in Systems and Being

The Absurdities Anthology
How Not to Find Your Local Weed-Man

The Gifted
The Untamed Force
Next Exit

The Shepherd Series
The Bad Shepherd
The Good Wolf

Standalone
Sundrops
Behind the Red Door
Boundless Fragments: A Collection of Novellas and Short Stories
Fragments of Forever

Watch for more at https://authorjasprings.com.

About the Author

I'm J. A. Springs.

Father of six wonderful children. I served twenty years on active duty, living around the world and experiencing things I never imagined I would. I spent time in societies and countries I once couldn't have envisioned as part of my future. I've done a lot—and still not enough.

These days, I live quietly, accompanied by my cats, music, and an interest in writing that consumes me. I've been writing seriously since 2021. I never set out to write in a particular genre—it made more sense to write around them instead. As for goals? There aren't many. Enjoy the first cup of coffee in the morning and see what the day brings.

Read more at https://authorjasprings.com.

About the Publisher

LLC. Lancaster, PA

www.writingfortheworldpress.com

Read more at https://www.writingfortheworldpress.com.